The Author

MORLEY CALLAGHAN was born in Toronto, Ontario, in 1903. A graduate of the University of Toronto and Osgoode Law School, he was called to the bar in 1928, the same year that his first novel, *Strange Fugitive*, was published. Fiction commanded his attention, and he never practised law.

While in university, Callaghan had taken a summer position at the *Toronto Star* when Ernest Hemingway was a reporter there. In April 1929, he travelled with his wife to Paris, where their literary circle of friends included Hemingway, Fitzgerald, and Joyce. *That Summer in Paris* is his memoir of the time. The following autumn, Callaghan returned to Toronto.

Callaghan was among the first writers in Canada to earn his livelihood exclusively from writing. In a career that spans more than six decades, he published sixteen novels and more than a hundred shorter works of fiction. Usually set in the modern city, his fiction captures the drama of ordinary lives as people struggle against a background of often hostile social forces.

Morley Callaghan died in Toronto, Ontario, in 1990.

THE NEW CANADIAN LIBRARY

MORLEY CALLAGHAN

Such Is My Beloved

With an Afterword by Milton Wilson

Reprinted 1991

Canadian Cataloguing in Publication Data

Callaghan, Morley, 1903–
Such is my beloved

(New Canadian Library)
Bibliography: p.
ISBN 0-7710-9955-X

I. Title. II. Series.

PS8505.A43S82 1989 C813'.52 C88-094965-1
PR9199.3.C343S82 1989

Typesetting by Pickwick
Printed and bound in Canada

McClelland & Stewart Inc.
The Canadian Publishers
481 University Avenue
Toronto, Ontario
M5G 2E9

To those times with M.
in the winter of 1933

Many waters cannot quench love, neither
can the floods drown it: if a man would
give all the substance of his house for
love, it would utterly be contemned.

– "Song of Songs"

One

THE MOST eager young priest at the Cathedral was Father Stephen Dowling. From the time of his ordination he had approached every bit of parish work with enthusiasm and preached with such passion that old Father Anglin, the pastor at the Cathedral, used to shake his head and wonder if the bishop could be advised to send him to some quite country town where he would not have to worry about so many controversial problems. It was rather disturbing for the older priest and some of the old and prosperous parishioners, too, to have a young man around who was apt to attack any difficult social problem with all the intensity of his very ardent nature. Last Sunday, for instance, at the ten o'clock mass, Father Dowling had preached a sermon on the inevitable separation between Christianity and the bourgeois world, and he spoke with a fierce warm conviction, standing in the pulpit and shaking his fist while his smooth black hair waved back from his wide white forehead and his cheeks were flushed from his glowing enthusiasm. After that sermon, Father Anglin had wanted to argue with the young priest, but he was afraid he would reveal too easily his own lack of faith in any social progress, so, instead of arguing, he merely stared at him with his pale blue eyes and shrugged his shoulders as a kind of warning.

Father Dowling was giving himself so eagerly to his work that he never stopped to wonder whether people approved of him. Besides, he had a charming smile that usually made everybody feel amiable, so he did not have to take criticism too seriously. Young people of the parish used to like him to come to their bridge parties. Older women loved to wait at the church door till he smiled a bit and then laughed out loud with a jolly burst of enthusiasm.

One night in the winter Father Dowling was returning from a visit to old Mrs. Schwartz who was sure, until he got to her bedside, that she was going to die. He had rushed to the house all ready to administer the last rites of the Church and he had bent over the old woman, listening to her moaning over and over that she did not want to die. He tried earnestly to soothe her. Then he began to be impressed with the vigor that was in the pious old woman's plea for life, and he smiled and felt sure that this time she would not die. After praying a while he began to talk to her in a loud, hearty voice; he assured her he would see her many times in church on Sundays, and then he went away.

He was on his way up the street by the theatres. The crowds were coming out. It had been snowing, the snow had suddenly turned to rain, but now the rain had stopped. Slush on the sidewalk was almost ankle deep. Father Dowling had his heavy woollen scarf up high around his neck. Young men and women huddled together for a while in the theatre entrance and then emerged under umbrellas as they rushed toward taxis. Father Dowling smiled at the way they stopped suddenly, looked up at the sky and then put down their umbrellas when they found there was no rain. From the corner he could look along the side street and see the Cathedral spire, but he did not look up, he turned mechanically, for he was carrying on in his head another powerful discourse on the building of a society on Christian principles and wondering if he dare use such fine bold thoughts in his next Sunday sermon. Some people would be stimulated enough to invite him to dinner for a further discussion: more prominent and wealthy parishioners would be sure to complain to Father Anglin and ask if it were wise to have a nice young fellow just a year out of the seminary bothering his head about such matters.

As he walked briskly by the hospital, he noticed two girls standing not far away from a lamp-post. One was tall with a dark red coat and a bit of scraggly gray fur around the neck; the other, the small one, was wearing a brown coat and a felt hat that had become shapeless after the rain. Father Dowling would have passed without ever looking at their faces, but the tall girl called, "Heh, where are you going? Wouldn't you like to stop a while?" Father Dowling's head shot up in surprise. Then he ducked his head and began to walk more rapidly, with his heart thumping hard. He only wanted to get out of their sight. But before he had gone twenty paces he began to be ashamed of his behavior, for he had ducked his head and hurried as though hiding some guilty thought or longing within him, or, in a way, it was as though he had turned up his collar and hidden from two wretched-looking girls who, no doubt, lived in his own parish not far away from the church. Turning he looked back, feeling ashamed, but wondering what he might have said to them. "At least I might have shown a little pity for them," he thought. Back at the corner the little girl, standing on one foot, held the other up as if it were wet and cold. Both girls were watching him. In spite of his timidity Father Dowling began to walk back slowly, and as he got closer to them he even managed to smile a little. With solemn, expressionless faces they stared at him, the big girl holding her withered fur collar up around her head to keep out the wind. He did not look like a priest with the muffler wrapped around his neck. Then the tall girl grinned and said suddenly, "Did you change your mind, Rosy Cheeks?"

"Eh, what's that?" Father Dowling said. The way she had spoken to him made him forget everything he had intended to say. He looked very severe as he said, "It's a terrible night to see you standing there. You ought to be home in some decent place out of this."

"You're right about that. We're not going to stand here much longer," the big girl said. "We're on our way now. Want to come, Rosy Cheeks?"

"Listen to me a moment, child."

But the little girl with the round, solemn face, who had been listening attentively, started to laugh and took hold of his arm. "Oh, come on. You want to come. Sure you want to come. I can tell you want to come."

Exasperated, Father Dowling pulled his arm away from her. He still wanted to be persuasive and patient, only now he was embarrassed. "You can't stand on the street corner like this. God knows what will happen to you in the long run. If you don't want to listen to me, go on your way home."

"Who said we didn't want to listen?"

"Sure we want to listen. Come on along and tell us all about it."

"Where are you going?"

"The Standard Hotel, Rosy Cheeks. It's just around the block."

"No, I can't do that," he said hastily.

"All right. If you can't, you can't, and there's no harm done. Some other time you may feel different. See what I mean? This is what I mean. Just ask for Ronnie any old time."

"Any old hour, we'll be awfully nice to you, Rosy Cheeks."

"You mustn't talk to me like that," he said, bending down angrily. He wanted to speak with earnestness and passion, but their sly, coaxing faces leering up at him made him feel confused, and suddenly, as he lost all confidence, he sighed, turned, and walked away rapidly with his head down and with contempt for himself. And he never looked back. His failure to be impressive with the girls made his face hot with shame. It was not yet clear to him what he ought to have done, but as he hurried to the church rectory he was full of sharp disappointment and more discouraged than he had been at any time since his ordination.

In the house he took off his hat and coat in a slow, thoughtful way, much worry showing in his sober face. Father Anglin, who was passing in the hall, stopped to offer the young priest a cigar that one of the parishioners had given to him. "It may explode in your mouth, but you like explosions, I believe," the old priest jested. "Thank you, thank you very much," Father Dowling said, and made no retort. As he went upstairs to his room, chewing the cigar, he was very worried, and when he sat down on the bed he was still twisting the unlighted cigar in his lips, for he couldn't stop thinking of the two girls on the corner, the serious, abrupt tall girl, the little one with the coaxing mouth and solemn eyes; they would be on the streets night after night and he had had an opportunity to help them and had failed. At this moment maybe they were in a cheap room in a low third-class hotel just on the other side of the block. Their rain-wet faces kept passing into his thoughts and he began to run his plump hand through his black hair, feeling dreadfully sad for the sake of their souls and full of pity because of the meanness of their lives. The more he pitied them and worried, the more vividly he saw them standing on the corner with the small one lifting her foot off the ground. "If I had been different, if there had been more warmth and understanding in me, those girls would have felt it. They would have wanted to listen to me. I would have touched them in some way," he thought. Through the noise of traffic on the streets and the long, shrieking whistle of a train down at the station, he still heard their voices and their mocking laughter. "Two girls in my own parish and in a hotel I could almost see from the window," he thought. And he got up eagerly and went to the window and pressed his smooth-shaven face against the cold glass, trying to see over roofs and chimneys, warehouses and backyards to the place where he knew the hotel was. But the water that had streamed down the window now blurred his vision. For a long time, though, he kept his face thrust against the pane, and all the time he was growing more dreadfully anxious. Then he felt an eagerness that made him turn suddenly from the window, full of confidence, and start to button up his vest. "I'll go over there and speak to them. Why shouldn't I call on them as I would on any one else in the parish who might need me?"

Father Dowling went out on tiptoe, and when he was on the sidewalk, going along the street, he smiled at his own nervousness. He knew he ought to tell another priest or even tell a policeman he was going to the girls' room, for fear of scandal developing, but he was more afraid this might lead to something that would cause the girls' arrest. It was necessary to have in mind some appropriate thoughts one might use in talking to such girls: the best he could do now as he put his head down against the wind was to half remember the sermon of an old missionary he had once heard preach to women at a mission. In the confessional it had always been easy for him to talk to women about moral looseness because they couldn't see him in the darkness and he could hardly see them. By this time he was on the other side of the block, in sight of the old hotel. The hotel, a three-storied yellow-brick building, was next door to an unlighted barber shop and a one-minute lunch counter. A broken electric sign with only a few of the letters lighted dimly, swung in the wind over the narrow hotel entrance.

Father Dowling began to make excuses to himself for his hesitant movements as he stood looking up at the sign, saying such things as, "I've passed this place many times. I've often wondered if the place did any business. I wonder who owns it?" or anything else he could think of that would permit him to delay. Then he took a deep breath, pulled his scarf high around his neck so no one would notice he was a priest and went bravely into the hotel. The lobby was small and dark. At the desk was a fat man with heavy, lifeless black hair with a rigid unnaturally white part in the middle and a very yellow dead-looking skin, who was apparently reading the newspaper spread out before him. He straightened up, readjusted the glasses on his almost bridgeless nose and eyed Father Dowling, who was smiling and making a little bow to him. The priest said, "There are two girls here I wanted to see. One is called Ronnie . . ."

"You want to see them, neighbor?"

"If you please."

"Then you sure can see them. Go on upstairs and rap on the first door to the right. It's a white door. Go up there, see." His short finger was pointing to the stair that had the edges of the steps protected with strips of brass. "Go up there, neighbor, and rap on the door."

As he went up the stairs Father Dowling wanted all the time to look back at the man at the desk. At the top he looked along the hall for the first door on the right, a white door. His heart began to beat more heavily as he went forward in the dimly lit hall. There was the faded gray-white door. And he rapped. But by the time the door was opened by the tall girl who had worn the red coat with the gray fur collar, he looked composed and very grave, and he nodded and said, "I've come to see you after all."

"I'll be jiggered if it ain't Rosy Cheeks himself, Midge. He's here after all. Come right on in."

"I think I will come in for a little while."

"I didn't say stay the night. You can't stay the night."

Father Dowling took off his hat and looked around slowly as if it were most important that he find a proper place to put it. He saw the room with the faded blue flowers on the wall-paper, the thick blue curtains on the window, the wide iron bed, painted white but chipped badly at the posts, and the copper-colored carpet that had a spot worn thin near the side of the bed. There were two chairs in the room. A door led into the next room. While he was looking around, the tall fair girl, who was wearing a loose blue dress that concealed the angularity of her body, assumed a ready smile, came over beside him and began to help him off with his coat with a dreadful efficiency. And the little, dark one with the round brown eyes and the smooth soft skin and a big bunch of black hair at the nape of her neck, jumped up from her chair with the same impressive efficiency, and in the affected manner of a great lady, extended her left hand with the elbow crooked as if he would be permitted just to touch the tips of her fingers. "How do you do, Sweetie. We are so mighty pleased to see you. You can't go wrong in coming here to see me."

"Who said he was coming to you?"

"He'll want to come to me. Won't you want to come to me?"

"Take it easy, Midge. Don't be so pushing. He doesn't want you. Why, he first spoke to me. You heard him speak to me. Hell, though, if Rosy Cheeks wants you, it's all the same to me."

"I'm not trying to rush him. Let him suit himself."

As Father Dowling listened, all the words from the sermon of the old missionary priest that had been in his head were forgotten, and by this time Ronnie, the tall one, was pulling off his scarf. Holding the scarf in her hand, she stood still. She saw his Roman collar and knew he was a priest. They both looked scared for a moment, then Ronnie said, "For the love of God, Midge, look what the wind blew in."

"He can't stay here. What are you going to do with him?"

"I didn't bring him. Maybe the poor guy wants to stay."

But Father Dowling had gained confidence in the one moment while the girls were abashed, so he waited to see what they would do. Starting to laugh, Ronnie said, "Don't get nervous, Father. It's all the same to us, you know," and her brisk, efficient manner returned, the grin settled on her face and she reached out in a hurry and took hold of his arm. Midge, who was slower to speak, had stepped back, frowning and timid; then she, too, grew bolder and she began to shake her shoulders till her full breasts swayed, and coming closer to him, she said, "Are you going for Ronnie, or do you want to leave it to me?"

"I'm sorry you didn't see I was a priest in the first place. I wanted to talk a while with you. After I left you I started to think about both of you. Please don't be impatient. If you're not going any place, I mean if you're in for the night let's sit down and talk."

"If you just want to talk why don't you hire a hall?"

"I'm not even anxious to talk, but I'd like to be friendly, and I won't tread on your toes either."

"Do you want to listen to his tall talk, Midge?"

"Oh, sure. Talk pays the rent. Let him talk himself right out the door and downstairs."

Then they stopped talking. They stared at him, half sneering. When he kept on waiting so patiently, they grew sullen and swung their heads away from him in disgust.

"Could I sit down a minute?" he asked. But still they would not answer. He sat down on one of the chairs, and then they looked at each other and Ronnie whispered, "Somebody may have tipped him off to come here, else he's a bit daffy," and since they could think of nothing else, they sat down on the bed. "We'd throw you out only you're the kind of guy that would start to holler," Midge said.

Father Dowling wiped his wide forehead with his handkerchief. His face, which was very young, pink and soft after the night air, still retained an expression of surprised innocence and still showed some of the eagerness that had brought him there. Grinning with embarrassment, he moistened his lips and said, "You'd let almost anybody else come here and talk to you. What's the matter with me? Can't we be friends?"

"I wish you'd get out quick, that's what I wish," Ronnie said.

"Go on, Father, please," Midge said.

"You don't have to be so harsh," he said, pleading with them and pleading with such earnestness that they began to feel tongue-tied.

"What's eating you, what's on your mind, Father?" Midge asked uneasily.

"It works out like this," he said. "You both looked mighty wretched standing there on the corner. It just struck me in such a way that I couldn't put the sight of you out of my mind, I guess. I never felt so much sympathy for anybody in my life. I wanted to do something to help you so you wouldn't want to stand on the streets like that."

"Say, are you going to sit here and listen to stuff like that, Midge?"

"You don't see the point, Ronnie," Midge said. "Father wants to keep us off the streets and if we don't listen to him he goes and calls a cop and then we're off the streets. See?"

"I won't call a cop."

"Aw, I'm tired," Ronnie said. "Go and peddle your pills next door. The lady of the house isn't in here." Ronnie waved her long thin arm threateningly. "Look here. We've got our own way of living just the same as you got yours." While Ronnie was speaking Midge got up and picked the priest's hat and coat and scarf off the chair and tossed them at him, saying, "Here, Father. Now get out of here quick before there's trouble."

"I had a great deal to say, don't be mean . . ."

"Run along, Father, and sell your papers," Ronnie said. Then she, too, got up and rushed over and took hold of the priest by the arm. Midge was reaching up trying to balance his coat and hat on his shoulder. The hat fell off on the floor. Father Dowling was humiliated, but the eagerness was so strong within him that he would not go and he said desperately, "Just one minute, one minute can't make any difference to you. Let me sit down just that long and then I'll go and there'll be no trouble."

"What do you want to sit down for?"

"Just to say a little prayer."

"For how long?"

"About a minute."

"And you'll get out then and not raise a noise? Go ahead."

So the two girls stood in front of Father Dowling on the threadbare carpet while he sat down on the chair, sighed and then looked up at them anxiously. The girls were motionless and wondering, for they couldn't understand his eager anxiety to be with them, nor could they understand his patience and gentle tolerance; and besides, he looked so much like a big awkward boy sitting there with his face smooth and pink, and somehow an expression of love in his eyes they had never seen before. He was calm, almost unaware of them, it seemed, as he made a small silent prayer. And when he had finished, he took a deep breath, smiled up at them and patted the back of his head with the palm of his strong right hand. "See there," he said. "I didn't do anybody any harm, did I? I just prayed that the grace of God will make things easier for you and you won't want to go out on the streets."

Thrusting her little black head forward so her full neck arched out of her plain black dress, Midge said suddenly, "What were you saying to yourself sitting there? Your lips weren't even moving. I was watching them."

"I wasn't talking to myself. In a way I was talking for you."

"You think you're doing a good turn for us, is that it?"

"I'd try very hard to help you."

"So you think we're pretty hopeless, eh, Father? Go on now. Say so."

"No, you don't seem low and you don't seem hopeless to me."

"Then why are you sitting there praying for us?"

"Maybe you're having a harder time than you imagine," he said timidly. "And without realizing it you may go from day to day making things harder till you yourselves lose all hope. That would be a dreadful time. There must be times now when you get up in the morning feeling full of despair, aren't there?"

"How about yourself in the mornings? Or is there always a little blue bird going tweet tweet tweet?" Ronnie said sharply.

"You're right. I need just as much help as you do. I'd love both of you to pray for me. To-night, when I get back to the Cathedral, I'll think about both of you and pray for you too." He smiled so charmingly that both girls felt ashamed of jibing at him. It was as though they both suddenly felt they could not help liking him, as though the warmth and eagerness that was in him had in some way reached them. His concern for them was so real that he stood there, worrying, wanting to say something, yet afraid of offending them. Midge, who was unable to take her eyes off his face, began biting her lips, and then she put the tips of two fingers up to her eye and she looked as if she might cry.

"What's the matter, child? Have I hurt you? I didn't want to say anything to offend you."

"You didn't. I guess I just feel a bit soft. You didn't hurt me."

"What's the matter, then?"

"Maybe it's the way you say things," she said.

The more stubborn and angular Ronnie glanced contemptuously at Midge, walked the length of the room and glanced bitterly at the priest. She had been holding her breath and now she released it noisily and she went over and sat beside Midge with her arm around her and said, "Never mind, kid. Don't get the jitters. What's got into you?" But she, herself, was looking worried.

When Father Dowling saw the girls moved in this way, he was so thankful his whole face beamed with gratitude. He moved his chair closer to the bed. He put his hand lightly and shyly on the little dark girl's head and stoked her hair softly and in him was a joy he had never known before. As he tried to smile at the two girls who had been moved by his presence, he felt more love for them than for any one he had known in his parish, a curious, new love that gave him a strange contentment. "Just let me sit here till you feel easier in your minds," he said. "Maybe you might tell me a little about yourselves."

Gradually he coaxed them to talk to him, drawing them out by showing a comradely interest in many practical matters. Ronnie answered briefly, with the gloomy expression still on her face. Almost everything this big awkward girl said seemed to hurt the priest so that he longed to say something witty or amiable that would make her more cheerful. Words began to come more readily from Midge.

She was a French-Canadian girl with a kind of flirtatious charm and many ridiculous, affected little mannerisms.

Finally he said, "We're friends now. Aren't we friends?"

"Yes, Father," they said. "We're good friends."

"That's splendid; that makes me feel fine. Don't you think I could help you to keep off the streets? Couldn't I try?"

"All right, Father," Midge said.

"How about you, Ronnie? It's a dreadful life you're leading."

But she shook her head gloomily, staring down at the floor as if she did not know how to abandon one way of living when she could see no way to turn afterwards.

"Is Ronnie your right name?" he asked.

"No. Veronica."

"Ah, that's a splendid Catholic name. I'm sure now that you were baptized. That's a great help. God bless you both, and this night, too."

As he put on his hat and coat he kept smiling with a kind of cheerful radiance, so happy he was, and by the time he placed his black hat firmly on top of his head, they too, were smiling shyly. "I'm coming back to see you, remember," he said. "I'll be back soon," and he went out the door leaving them standing side by side in the room.

This time, going down the stairs, Father Dowling almost forgot he was in a hotel, and he did not look at the proprietor, Mr. H.C. Baer, who was still reading the paper at the desk. But Mr. Baer, jerking his glasses rapidly up to the bridge of his nose, saw the white priest's collar which Father Dowling thought was still hidden by the woollen muffler, and he grinned so broadly that the corners of his wide mouth seemed to shoot up to his skull, he glanced up the stairs, and he made a loud sneering noise with his heavy wet lips.

Outside it had got much colder. The weather had been very changeable all over the East this last week. It was now starting to snow. Walking had become difficult because of the frozen ruts in the slush on the sidewalk. But Father

Dowling was in no hurry. His feeling of great joy was so astonishing that he wanted to hold on to it and meditate upon it till it was completely understood. He began to walk much slower, putting first one hand then the other up to his tingling red ears. As he turned the corner and saw first the spire of the Cathedral and then the dark mass of the old weather-beaten structure, hemmed in closely by office buildings and warehouses and always dirtied by city soot, and with the roof now covered with snow and moonlight shining on the white slope, Father Dowling felt a fresh full contentment.

In the hall of the rectory where he was kicking off his rubbers for the second time that night, he heard only one sound, a cough coming from old Father Anglin's study at the head of the stairs. The other priest, young Father Jolly, was in bed. As he started to climb the stairs, Father Dowling wondered if he ought to discuss the girls with Father Anglin, and as he deliberated, he could see in his thoughts the old priest turning slowly from the desk and listening patiently. Father Anglin was, of course, a very pious old priest, white-haired, fresh-faced, vigorous too, although a bit settled in his habits and way of thinking. Everybody in the neighborhood, storekeepers, Italian fruit dealers, Jewish tradesmen, Protestant business men and the policemen on the corners all knew the old priest. Every afternoon he walked out in his gray and shabby coat and his big body rolled along the street with his wide black hat square on top of his white head and bobbing up and down like a cork on a wave. Bits of hair stuck out at the sides of his hat, his face was always red as if he couldn't get his breath, and half the time his eyes seemed to be closed. At four o'clock in the afternoon he went forth to his favorite coffee-shop where he sat down without removing his hat and ordered and ate with a deep expansive relish a club sandwich containing dainty bits of chicken breast and bacon and tomato and lettuce and toasted bread and two dill pickles. Everybody in the place stared at him because he looked so sober. He felt just as sober as he looked. At a marriage time in his church he was hostile to what he called pagan celebrations because he said marriage was a sacrament and therefore a serious business and so he was opposed to having rice thrown frivolously at the door of the church. Moreover, no marriage ceremony was performed later than eight o'clock in the morning.

When Father Dowling reached the top of the stairs, he was seeing Father Anglin so vividly in his thoughts that he stood still, pondered a bit longer, lapping his lower lip over his long upper one, and said to himself, "Father Anglin has a beautiful Christian character, no doubt, but somehow I don't think he would like to hear me talking about those girls."

So he went to his own room, and before he went to bed he prayed for a long time for the souls of Ronnie and Midge. He prayed that he might have the full care of their souls so he could safeguard them. But the best part of his prayer was when he was absolutely silent and very calm, and he could see Ronnie and Midge standing close together in the hotel room, dogged and puzzled. And he was so moved that when he got into bed he felt that his feeling for the girls was so intense it must surely partake of the nature of divine love.

Two

THE SECOND time Father Dowling went to see the two girls in the hotel was the evening of the first Thursday in February. All evening he had been hearing confessions. He sat in the confessional with his elbow on the rail by the grating, with the faint musk-like priest odor pervading the confessional box, listening tirelessly to girls and old men, and giving himself sympathetically to their sorrow for the slightest sin. But after an hour and a half he grew very weary. The last confession he heard was from a young hysterical girl who seemed to him to be making up a chain of small sins so that she could imagine herself full of remorse. Growing exasperated, he thrust his face against the wire grating and said sharply, "My goodness, child, you're entitled as a human being to certain judgments about your fellow creatures. Every time you have an opinion about your neighbor you're not committing a mortal sin. Don't you understand that?" The girl was startled by his face and breath and moving lips so close to her, and dropping her head down in the darkness she whispered, "Yes, Father, I understand." Then she seemed unable to lift her head. Father Dowling, giving her absolution very quickly, wondered whether he should explain that a priest ought not to be worried by such trifles, but he smiled as he saw her standing up hurriedly, and when she swung aside the curtain and went out he leaned back with relief.

For a long time he waited and no one entered the confessional. He waited and reflected on the young girl's imagined sorrow, her fictitious sin and her fancied penitence, and he suddenly remembered the two girls, Midge and Ronnie. It seemed to him sitting there silently in the darkness, with one hand twisting the end of the purple stole around his neck, that there had been something very beautiful and real about their regret that night in the hotel room, with Midge biting her lip and crying and Ronnie's face full of dogged despair. It seemed astonishing yet consoling that human beings so fettered in degradation could rise so swiftly when moved by simple friendliness. Father Dowling was suddenly eager to see them again.

After waiting twenty minutes longer, he went out to the aisle and looked up and down at the almost empty church, where a few women were saying their penance up at the front by the altar rail. No one was sitting on the penitent's bench waiting to go into the confessional. He walked rapidly up the aisle and across the altar, genuflecting before the tabernacle, and then crossed through to the sacristy.

When he was dressed and out on the street, he felt a peculiar exhilaration and joy in life and his work in the parish. It was a very clear, cold night, with a brilliantly starred, far-away winter sky. His feet scrunched on the snow. All of his work since his ordination, as he thought of it, seemed groping and incomplete unless the way he had helped Midge and Ronnie was included, too. It seemed to him now, going along the street with a long swinging stride and his hands in his pockets, that his prayers for these girls would never be unheeded. He smiled very happily to himself.

He was on the other side of the block, walking more slowly and wondering if it would be better to pull his scarf up high around his neck so he would not be recognized as a priest when he came in sight of the hotel. In one way he hated any such deception. Yet he knew that he ought to avoid giving scandal in the presence of ignorant stupid people, who were ever anxious to sneer at the Church. For a moment he stopped on the other side of the street, opposite the barber shop, giving himself a little more time to decide whether he would conceal his collar, while he looked at the dimly lighted hotel entrance. Then he saw a girl coming up the street and when she passed under the light he knew it was Ronnie with her red coat and the bit of gray fur on the collar, but he stood there without moving because he noticed her glancing over her shoulder twice at a short, wide-shouldered man in a peak cap who was following her, and when she got to the hotel, she made a slight motion with her head toward the door, waited till he got closer, and then went in with the man in the peak cap right behind her. This happened so very quickly, so furtively, that Father Dowling, who was across the street, did not seem to understand its meaning. "That was the tall girl, Ronnie, all right," he thought, while his heart beat heavily and he grew dreadfully uneasy. "God help her for her shamelessness," he thought, growing angry. Up and down and back and forth he paced, feeling a rage within him. It seemed terrible that a mortal soul that he had loved and prayed for was being degraded almost within reach of him while he stood helpless on the street. It was this helplessness, so much deeper within him than his anger, that he could not understand, and bit by bit this helplessness possessed him till soon his anger was completely submerged.

In a surprisingly short time there was a shadow in the hotel door across the road. The man with the peak cap came out, looked up and down very carefully, stood long enough to light a cigarette and then began to loaf down the street with a slow contented rolling gait and an air of complete well-being. Father Dowling hated him, feeling big and strong enough to beat him. All his mixed-up anger and disappointment grew into a steady hatred of this man who loafed along lazily till out of sight. Father Dowling thought of rushing into the hotel and speaking to Ronnie, but the notion of going into the room so shortly after such a man had glutted himself and left disgusted him. "I'll wait just a little longer. I'll walk up the street a bit and maybe she'll come out," he thought, pretending he was not cold and that the weather was very mild, when his ears were actually red and tingling and even his hands thrust deep in his pockets felt cold. His feet, too, were chilled, and hurt him when he moved and the blood began to circulate again.

He had almost decided it would be better to return to the church and possibly visit the hotel the following afternoon when he saw Midge crossing the road. There was just enough light slanting from the broken sign over the hotel door to shine on her tilted face, which was smiling up coaxingly at the very heavy, respectable, sober-faced man of middle age who was on her arm. She did not go into the hotel furtively. She did not walk ahead of the man as Ronnie had done. She was hanging on his arm as if she had known him intimately for years, and had always given him an abundant happiness out of her own deep love. If it had not been for the anxious expression on the gray middle-aged man's face they might have looked like a pair of lovers.

Father Dowling felt a little weary. Midge and her man passed not twenty feet away from him. At first he thought the disgust in him was for this mean hotel and the girls, but then it became, too, a weariness and disgust for himself as he remembered how he had felt sure that his presence and his eagerness had meant very much that other night to the two girls. It seemed now like a kind of rare conceit that had been making him, even in his prayers, feel joyful and sure of himself. At most he ought only to have dared to hope and prayed very humbly. Instead he had been going around smiling happily at everybody as if he had a secret that neither other priests nor parishioners would ever understand.

But he waited till he saw the middle-aged man in the gray coat come hurriedly out of the hotel, pull his hat down far over his eyes and start to walk furtively up the street, gradually increasing his pace and almost running as if expecting to be arrested at any moment, or to have some one touch him on the shoulder and point back at the hotel.

Father Dowling crossed over and entered the hotel. He did not even look at the man at the desk. He went straight to the stair with the bits of brass on the edges. His face was full of sober earnestness and there was a peculiar dignity about the way he carried his head. His scarf was high up around his neck, though he was so little concerned he never wondered whether the desk man noticed him. But Mr. Baer's glasses were thrust up on the bridge of his nose, the head with heavy woodenly arranged hair shot forward, and grinning with his thick underlip tight against his teeth, he said to himself, "There goes the lamb of God again. I wonder which one he likes. Probably the little one. I'll ask her about him. He's the best-looking customer she ever had. More power to her good right arm."

Father Dowling rapped on the white door at the head of the stairs, and when it was opened a few inches, he said mildly, "May I come in?"

"Lordy, it's Father. Hello, Father." He could just see the lower part of Ronnie's jaw, the lighted tip of a cigarette and a cloud of smoke. "Come on in," she said.

He nodded gravely. Midge, who was sitting on the chair where he had sat the other night, had on a very loose blue dress, like a slip. Her hair was done in curls on her neck. As soon as she saw the priest she stood up, making her little bow and putting out her left hand with the elbow extended from her body. "Hello, Father, how are you?" she said.

"You won't mind sitting on the bed, will you, Father?" Ronnie said. Both girls were feeling good-humored, almost exhilarated, with their rouged cheeks flushed and their eyes full of animation. Ronnie, standing up with a good-natured grin on her stubborn face, pointed to the bed. "Sit down. How've you been, Father?" she said. He dreaded sitting on that bed, but finally he sat down, and was unable to do anything but stare at them severely. His big strong hands were lying heavily on his knees. His face looked white and full of uneasiness.

"You don't look so cheerful, so chirpy tonight, Father," Midge said. She seemed really concerned. "You look as if you'd been working at something too hard," she said.

"What's the matter with you, Father. You're sitting there like an extra bed-post," Ronnie said irritably.

"Tell me this," he said with sudden anger. "Didn't my coming here the other night mean anything to you at all?"

"It sure did," Midge said. "Do you know, Father, I couldn't get to sleep at all that night. Honest to God I couldn't. I kept wanting to talk to Ronnie. I'd keep waking up and nudging her till she wanted to crown me."

"Didn't you regret the life you were leading?"

They didn't answer him. The sullen dogged expression was on Ronnie's face and Midge kept shifting her glance away, trying to avoid the priest's angry eyes. But they did not look like persons aware of guilt. They were merely uneasy and resentful, as if they did not want to listen. Sometimes Midge looked directly at him with a bold impatience and he saw she was pretty, and remembered how she had taken the middle-aged man into the hotel half an hour ago. "I was on the street and I saw you both come in here with men," he said quietly, without any anger, just as if stating a fact. "I stood there, waiting till the men came out. I know both of you. You don't understand the anxiety a priest can feel for two girls like you. It was terrible to have to stand out there and know what was going on up here."

"You might as well get off your high horse, Father. There's no use talking to us like that," Ronnie said.

"I'm on no high horse. I'm not talking down to you. I'm talking about something that happened."

Ronnie was now sitting on the arm of Midge's chair with her hand on the smaller girl's shoulder. There was something Father Dowling admired in the direct and simple gestures of this big girl with the businesslike manner and the blunt speech. "Now see here, both of you, I'm not trying to be harsh," he said. "Only I have been praying a lot for you and I thought I had really touched you in some way the other night. . . ."

"Oh, don't keep nagging at us," Midge said. "Why do you come here if you want to nag us?"

"What's that, my child? I don't want to nag you."

"You have a good time talking about praying for us, don't you, but prayers won't pay for our room, prayers won't help me get my hair curled. You can't eat prayers. How do you think we're going to live? Did you ever stop to figure that out?"

"There are millions of girls with decent jobs. You seem full of bitterness."

"There are more girls than jobs. What are you going to do with the girls left over? And this is the middle of a cold winter, too."

"Isn't it better to starve than lose your . . ."

"If that's what's worrying you and if it will buck you up and make us seem like tin saints, we're just about starving now. Look around this dump. See all the silks and satins. What do you see? See that old brown coat of mine over there? I've been wearing it for three years. I have to take it off like it was tissue paper or it'll fall to pieces. Isn't this a lovely room? Don't you hate to put your wet boots on that lovely rug? It's filthy, filthy, filthy, but I'd rather be here than out there," she said, pointing to the window. The little dark girl was pouring the words out of her as if she had become full of hate. "We're not even high-class whores, see," she said. "We take what comes our way and mighty glad to get it." She was speaking with all the fury of an indignant, respectable woman and the mingling of her strange humility and her passion was so convincing that Father Dowling began to feel doubtful, as if there might be many things he did not understand. He could see the twisted heels on Ronnie's shoes, the broken toe-cap, and the stockings with the sewn-up runs. A long time ago he had heard a Redemptorist priest preaching a sermon about the luxurious life of vice which was always a temptation to poor girls. Somehow, he himself had always thought of vice as yielding to the delights of the flesh, as warmth and good soft living and laziness. But as he looked around this room and at these angry girls he felt close to a dreadful poverty that was without any dignity. He felt, too, that Ronnie and Midge worked far harder than almost any young women he knew. Bewildered, he said, "I don't want to seem stupid. I don't want to abuse you, either. There's no more degraded an existence than yours, but, listen, don't be impatient with me. I'm not sure I'm wise enough to blame you. Perhaps there are many things I don't altogether understand. I know it's hard to be hungry and be a Christian. I understand that."

"You bet your boots you can understand that. We can understand anything that touches our bellies."

"Oh, she doesn't hate you, Father. Don't get excited, Midge."

"Why should she hate me, Ronnie?"

"She doesn't hate you. She's just up in the air. Take it easy, Midge."

"I'll hate him if I want to. I hate everybody in the whole damned lousy world," Midge said, jumping up from her chair, her round brown eyes brilliant with indignation. "I'll hate his old man and his old woman and his whole damned family if I want to. See." But she saw Father Dowling smiling very gently, as if her indignation was so honest he couldn't help liking it. She grew quiet and after looking at him for a moment, she smiled a bit too, and said, "I guess I'm flying off the handle, Father."

Father Dowling was smiling because he felt some of his eagerness returning. There was much he had not understood, there was a whole economic background behind the wretched lives of these girls. They were not detached from the life around them. They had free will only when they were free. He remembered suddenly, with a quick smile that brightened his face, how he had learned in the seminary that St. Thomas Aquinas has said we have not free will when we are completely dominated by passion. Hunger was an appetite that had to be satisfied and if it was not satisfied it became a strong passion that swept aside all free will and rational judgment. If he properly understood the lives of these girls, he thought, he might realize they were not free but strongly fettered and he would not be so sure of judging them. And as if he were longing for some explanation that might restore his hope for the girls, he decided that he must first try and help them to live decently. He looked at them warmly and moistened his lips.

"What did you use to do?" he asked Ronnie.

"I worked in a department store. It wasn't steady work, though."

"Didn't you like it?"

"Sure, only I'm telling you, I only worked part time."

"Wouldn't you like a decent job now?"

"Try and get me one."

"I certainly will try," he said.

He leaned back on the bed, almost at ease now, and began to ask Midge about Montreal, where she had lived, and how many children there were in the family. Smiling at him, as if she thought him very funny, she said there were twelve children in her family. She started to name them all. "Louise, George, Henry, Theresa," then she stopped, frowned very seriously, tried to get the children in the right order of their emergence into life, giggled, and began to count slowly on her fingers. "How many's that?" But when she had finished naming all the children and had described how their mother had managed to feed them all properly, she explained that she had left home with a fellow she had thought might possibly marry her. He had definitely promised to at the time. Then she was silent, reflective, frowning, trying to understand many things about those times, years ago.

She was silent so long that Father Dowling coughed, then laughed boyishly and began to explain that he had come from a country town up around the lakes. There had only been, as far as he could remember, his mother and one brother, and they had had a hard time putting him through the seminary. He could not remember his father, though he had a picture of him in his bureau drawer. It was always a satisfaction, it was more than that, it was delightful to see his mother and brother in the town when he went home for a holiday. They wanted to parade him into every neighbor's home. His mother strutted around the main street and in the stores with her chest thrown out looking and talking like a bishop. Indeed, since his ordination, she had become the town bishop and was very severe about every one's morals. Father Dowling started to laugh, a rolling hearty laugh, and Ronnie and Midge laughed too. Soon they were all feeling jolly and friendly. They kept on talking till Father Dowling heard the sound of wheels on the frozen road, the squeaking of iron wheels on hard snow echoing on the clear night air. "My goodness, it can't be the milk wagon, can it?" he said, and he got up to go.

But when he had his hat and coat on he became very embarrassed and even blushed. Resolutely he put his hand in his pocket and took out a bill-fold. "I'm going to try and get jobs for you," he said. "Won't you let me help you until then?" He took two five-dollar bills, all there was in the bill-fold, and said, "Please take this. I know you won't go on the streets if you don't need money. Isn't that true? At least the strongest temptation will be gone. Please take it." He was actually pleading with them.

Midge looked at Ronnie. Both girls grinned. "Thanks, Father," Ronnie said. "My goodness. You must excuse anything we've said. I had no idea – we did not expect anything like this. It's mighty decent of you."

"Oh, thank you, Father. You're a peach," Midge said.

"Now, good night, both of you. Think of me. Keep trying hard, and if you could only say a little prayer . . . well, never mind. Good night."

Father Dowling went downstairs. This time, as he passed the desk, he did not like the way the proprietor smiled. There was a kind of leering comprehension in the smile that disturbed him.

But when he was outside in the clear night air, he knew it was very late. "My goodness," he said and began to rush home. He was already planning whom he might ask to find jobs for the girls. Then suddenly he wondered if he ought to have given them money. He tried to define the objection to giving them money, but it remained too deeply hidden within him.

Three

THE NEXT night Ronnie and Midge left the hotel at about ten o'clock. Ronnie went one way, on the side streets, and Midge went over to the brightly lighted neighborhood by the theatres.

With the money Father Dowling had given her Midge had bought herself a new brown felt hat which she wore tilted pertly on one side of her head. To-night she was feeling hopeful. There was a little animation in her face that came from feeling sure that she looked attractive. As soon as she was on the avenue she began to walk more slowly, stopping a long time at each interesting shop window to look at hats and lingerie and expensive hose, and peering with one eye at the window mirrors to see if any one was standing beside her. This last month had been a difficult one. It had been cold. Most of the men who might have picked her up were out of work. So she walked on down the street, her eyes swinging to the left and right, staring into faces coming toward her without ever moving her head, waiting eagerly for some faint intimation from some one that he had been attracted. All the men seemed to be walking rapidly with their heads down, their breath vaporing out on the cold air, men with black mustaches and full, ruddy faces and tall, slim, cold-looking men. Midge began to rub her hands together. The old kid gloves were thin. For the first part of the evening she would hope desperately that it would not be necessary to speak to any one and that some fellow of his own accord would follow her. Night after night, especially now in the winter, when so few seemed interested in her, it was getting harder and harder to speak to them when she knew they would refuse. When they kept on shaking their heads it got so that she did not expect them to want her.

Then she began to feel cold; hardly any one seemed to be on the street, so she went into a corner restaurant to have a cup of coffee. The hot coffee warmed her. Feeling more hopeful, she sat at the table demurely. The crowds would soon be coming out of the theatres.

If it had not been for her shabby clothes and a slyness in her eyes, Midge might have looked wistful, sitting at the white-topped table in the almost deserted restaurant. Four years ago she had been living in Montreal. She had been the oldest girl in their large family, and her mother and father had expected her to stay at home and help with the house and children. In the afternoon she had got into the habit of walking down by the docks and the riverside and looking at the ships from strange places and hearing the rough voices of seamen shouting in a language she did not understand. She used to look for a long time at the immense blueness of the wide St. Lawrence, flowing with such a dreadful steadiness toward the open sea. Down by the waterfront men laughed and spoke to her and hollered after her when she hurried away, full of excitement. At home her mother always seemed to be sick, or preparing for another child. Midge did the housework and dreamed of the streets at the waterfront, and the streets full of noise and shouting by the warehouses, and the streets by the big hotels in the evening.

Her first lover, a boy out of work named Joseph, took her to the all-night cafés and got her for his girl that winter, and she came to see him every afternoon. Her mother used to look at her sorrowfully when she went out on those afternoons, as if she knew all that was happening to her daughter, but was afraid to remonstrate for fear of driving her away from home.

Then she left Montreal with a lover named Andy, who lived with her for two months. They had been very much in love, she thought at the time. He used to run his hand through her black hair. They used to walk together in the fine spring evenings, with him smiling down into her face and holding her arm so tight, walking in the spring evenings all around the city parks and out by the lakeshore, making plans, following the crowds. And when he left her she was wild with resentment. For a time she was without any feeling. The first man that wanted her took her, a friend of Andy's, though she could hardly remember that time with him. Looking back, that friend of Andy's hardly seemed a part of her life, she could hardly remember his name. And after that no one stayed with her very long, but she went from one to another for a place to live.

The rich odors of cooking food and the hot coffee warmed Midge as she sat alone in the restaurant. She smiled to herself, for she thought suddenly of Father Dowling's eager, earnest face. "He's very nice. There's a lot of fun in him. I wonder if he's got much money? He looked very happy last night when he went out. Maybe we ought not to laugh at him. I wonder whether he likes me better than Ronnie?" she thought. And she went on smiling and liking the worried expression that had been on Father Dowling's face and the deep rolling laugh that burst out of him when he talked about his mother and his home.

When she went out again, she looked up and down the street carefully. She saw the crowds beginning to come out of the theatre. She watched to see which way most of them were going and then sauntered toward them. There was a policeman standing on the corner across the street and she had to keep watching him all the time as he thumped his arms across his chest and stood far back in the doorway out of the cold wind. Then a young fellow with huge shoulders, who idled along with his overcoat open as though it were a hot summer evening, stared at her boldly when she passed, so she smiled ever so slightly and walked a little slower. By this time she could almost feel when a man turned around and was coming after her. She walked on without turning her head till she came to a drug store with a wide window, and she entered and sat down all alone at the counter, looking out at the street. The young fellow with the big shoulders stood on the pavement where he could see her, and when she smiled coaxingly he came in eagerly and sat down beside her. In this way she made him feel that he really knew her. They had a cup of coffee together. He had a short snub nose and many freckles and he looked like a laborer who was dressed up in his best clothes for an evening's amusement. He was not at all shy and had a full generous smile. And by the time they left the drug store she was hanging on to his arm, he was holding her hand possessively as though she were his girl, and she kept on smiling up at him all the way over to the hotel, where he handled her with tremendous satisfaction till she was forced to make him think she was exhausted. Laughing and full of conceit, he gave her two dollars, then frowned, hesitated, wondering if he ought to give her more, and instead, he swore he would come and see her at the same time next week.

But all the rest of that evening no one would glance at Midge. She tried whispering as she passed by, she nodded her head, she walked alongside them while her face and feet and hands got cold. She went far out of her usual way and down by the station where all the taxis were lined up at the curb, but the wide street was almost deserted. People kept getting out of cars and rushing into the station. Across the road the great face of the hotel gleamed with light. She kept on going over by the market and finally she went back to her own neighborhood by the theatres. With her shoulders hunched up, she was standing on the corner looking idly at the snow that was beginning to fall in big, heavy, wet flakes on the almost deserted streets. The slowness of the slanting snow made her feel all the more discouraged. But then she picked up the worried young man with the thin face, the little dark mustache and the big horn-rimmed glasses, who was a student, and she took him home on her arm. But he wanted to sit in the room with the blue curtains and talk to her, and she kept on trying to get him to go into the other room. "Come on and play house. Don't you want to play house?" she kept on coaxing. But he only smiled and twisted uneasily on his chair, trying to conceal his fear of her and hoping to make up his mind while he kept on putting her off. "I'll tell you what," he said suddenly. "Take off your clothes and do a dance for me."

A bit bewildered, she looked at him and then hated him and sneered. "What do you think this is? What's the matter with you?"

"What difference does it make to you what you do?"

"It makes a lot of difference. What do you think I am?"

"God, aren't you proud!"

"I can't dance," she said sullenly.

"Go ahead and try. I'll pay you anyway."

"I know what you are. You're a college boy, and you don't know any better."

"What are you so stuck up about? What do you care what you do?"

"What do you think this is, a roadhouse? You get the hell out of here," she yelled at him. With a grin of relief on his face, he hurried out, thumbing his nose at the door, and when she was alone she was so indignant and full of rage that she kept on pacing up and down the room. She felt helpless with resentment. She started to cry. There was no use going out again. It was after midnight. Ronnie was not coming home; she was staying the night with Lou. So Midge went over to the window and looked out, feeling lonesome, and the streets seemed so clear and cold that she shivered and wrote something with her finger on the frosted pane. "Maybe the priest might come along the street and stay and talk a while," she thought. The church was just on the other side of the block. But no matter how she strained her neck she could not see the spire. "He would have been glad to see the way I chased that little college boy out of the room," she thought, smiling. There would have been something about it that would have pleased him. It was almost as though she had done something for him, and it was more likely that he would give her money the next time he came to the hotel.

Four

RONNIE did not work the streets the way Midge did. There were times when she used to hate to see Midge leaning sentimentally on some fellow's arm, smiling up into his face and making him think she loved him. Of course, Midge, in this way, had men coming back to her all the time, but Ronnie, though, was full of contempt for such men who wanted to be petted and coaxed. That evening at ten o'clock she went out; she kept to the side streets, away from the big avenues, avoiding the crowds and the corners where the policemen walked most often. In her old red coat she looked like an ordinary, practical working girl, except that her lips were too red and her eyes were made up badly, and while she walked rapidly she kept quite warm. Every man who came toward her she estimated shrewdly, seeking the ones who were idling along, for she never expected a man to approach her. To-night she kept to the darker streets in the block behind the Cathedral, where there were a great many old rooming houses. When her hands began to feel stiff with the cold she took off her gloves and put her fingers in her mouth and blew her hot breath on them, but when she took her fingers out of her mouth her hand looked red and beefy. The sharp dry coldness without any wind went right through her, because she could not wear too many clothes. Whenever a man was passing her she said, "Hello, kiddo," and if he slowed down, she said, "I know a warm place for such a cold night."

Ronnie had come from Detroit ten years ago with her father. In Detroit, in those days, times had been good, but there had been a jealousy between her father and mother that developed into a hatred, and when they were divorced they took turns having Ronnie live with them. They just used her as a means of hurting each other. They both insisted on having her and really didn't want her at all. Her father, when he had her with him, used to look at her morosely and wonder what to do with her. Her mother, when she had her, used to spend a lot of time trying to find out secrets about the father. So Ronnie became sullen and reticent with both of them and waited for the time when she would be old enough to live by herself.

One time she refused to return to Detroit and she got a job in a department store and a small room of her own. Those days, at first, were the best ones of her life. She lived frugally; she tried to save a little money; she had a splendid independence. But they shortened her hours at the department store; her pay envelope kept getting thinner till soon she was only working a few hours a week and not making enough to pay her room rent. It was then that she found out it was easy to attract men passing through the store and make dates with them for an hour or two later, when she would not be working. She began by accepting small presents that went toward paying for her food and rent.

To-night, as she was walking up toward the Garden, where there was a boxing match, she saw a fat, middle-aged man coming down the street with his fur-lined coat swinging open. He was smoking a big cigar and his hat was cocked on one side of his head and when she spoke to him, he said, "O.K. with me, sister. What have you got to offer? I'd just been wondering if there wasn't any whoring in this town. You go out looking for a woman and you're apt to pick up a policeman. Never saw such a dump. I'm from the West." And Ronnie said considerately, "Maybe you'll want to just follow me. It will look better." She always made this suggestion because so many men were nervous and kept looking around with such anxiety and fear of being observed that they attracted the attention of passing people. They felt so much more respectable just following Ronnie to the hotel, where it was never necessary for any one to stay with her more than twenty minutes.

But the bland gentleman, who was almost without passion, could hardly be coaxed to put down his cigar. He was a railroad man and he wanted to tell her about a hundred cities in a hundred places all over the continent. "I know fifty good guys like myself who'll be glad to see you when they come here. Danged if you won't set them up," and he wrote down her name with a stubby pencil in a big black notebook which he kept in his hip pocket.

When the railroad man had left she hurried back to her best neighborhood, and the next one was a boy who was dreadfully shy, and only had a dollar. This boy with curly fair hair, who went to high school, seemed to think she was wonderful, and he was very timid, so she was kind and patient with him, so good-natured, in fact, that he wanted to stay in the room with her and talk with great eagerness. But he left like the others in twenty minutes.

After that, no matter how far away from her own neighborhood she walked, no one would speak to her, no one would turn when she reached out and touched an arm: they kept on passing, sometimes looking down at her face, shrugging their shoulders and hurrying on to their homes with their hands in their pockets. Hundreds of mysterious faces of hundreds of people, long hungry faces, full round faces with black mustaches, foreign faces, hard, bitter faces, all coming along the side streets from the shows, passed by, cold and solemn, some of them turning just long enough to glance at her appraisingly. Because of the cold, it was necessary to walk fast and so her thoughts were teeming full of these many faces, and full, too, of an increasing dread of the next new face, as if one more refusal would break something inside her. She was a stubborn girl, so she kept thinking, "Jees, they can't hurt me. It's all the same to me," and yet she could not stop herself from staring sullenly at every man who passed, and growing warm with hate. It was at this time that the wet, heavy snow began to fall and drift across the street light. She stopped, looking up at the sky, and wondered where Midge was and why she hadn't met her all evening. She wondered if the falling snow would make Midge decide to go back to the hotel. "If it snows heavily to-night, it will be warmer to-morrow, maybe," she thought. The corner grocery store was still lighted. Peering through the window at the clock, she said, "Goodness, twenty to twelve. Lou will be waiting for me if I don't hurry," and she began to hurry back to the hotel like a girl who is eager to get home after the day's work is over.

She stayed in the hotel only long enough to powder her face and pat her hair and take with great care from the bureau drawer a neat bundle which she tucked under her arm. And this time when she went out, she wasn't interested in any one who passed her. She looked ahead eagerly.

She saw Lou walking up and down slowly on the corner opposite the bank building, a lighted cigarette in his gloved hand. Lou was a little fellow in a dark overcoat and a derby hat, who leaned back a little so he would look taller, and who glanced contemptuously at almost everybody who passed by, so he could feel he was nursing his own strength and feel he was a bad man for any one to tangle with on a street at night. His face was soft and pallid, but his eyes were really hard and colorless. Three years ago he had been a shoe clerk. That was before he had met Ronnie. His father and mother, who had wanted him to become a business man, had thought the shoe business a good one for an industrious young fellow who was willing to learn rapidly and work hard, but the monotony of the life had begun to bore him. In the noon hours he had begun to go to the pool parlors. He began to bet on the horses, and he quit his job.

Lou appreciated Ronnie's good qualities and was very kind to her. Whenever she was sick, he insisted she go to the hospital at once. If she got into trouble with a policeman, he knew a lawyer who would rush to the station and arrange a small bail bond for her. For a holiday he sometimes took her to the country. And he kept on sending men to the hotel and telling them to be sure and ask for Ronnie and not to bother with the little dark girl, whom he did not like.

It did not seem cold to Ronnie as she walked along the street with Lou; the tingling night air only made her feel more alive. All the stubborn aloofness that had seemed a part of her nature disappeared. Laughing, she walked along, holding Lou's arm tight, feeling his body swaying from side to side with his swagger while he talked out of the corner of his mouth. His rooming house was just by the bridge over the river and the railroad tracks. Across the bridge, on the other bank, behind the factories, they could see the jail, and they could see the reflections of street lights on the snow on the frozen river below. Sometimes an automobile light gleamed on the railroad tracks by the river and on the rows of boxcars, white capped with snow, more numerous further down by the dark waterfront and the bay. There was a long and lonely cry of an engine and the clanging of a bell, and a passenger train came rushing toward the bridge with its coaches gleaming with light and life and swift glimpses of men with their hats off, drummers and farmers and city men, relaxing on the green seats, quick glimpses of a thousand people never to be seen again as the swaying coaches roared under the bridge, going far north and points west on the continent with a rapid flickering of window life – then the darkness, the bare tracks, the river, the freight-yard, the boxcars, the factories and chimney stacks again.

"Don't you love it?" Ronnie asked. "Going right under your feet and going the Lord knows where."

"Maybe it's going north."

"Maybe it's going to Montreal where Midge comes from."

"Maybe it's going to the Pacific Coast. You can't say for sure."

"Gee, wouldn't you like to be on that train, Lou?"

"We'll take a trip some day, kiddo. Leave it to me."

"Every time I see a train I want to be going away," she said.

Lou had a big front room in an old house with long, poorly lit halls and great high ceilings. When they entered this room, they took off their coats eagerly, tossing them over the furniture like people who were glad to be in their own house. Hiding the parcel she had been carrying under the folds of her coat, she ran to the gas stove at the end of the room, lit the gas, took the coffee pot down from the shelf and began to work busily like a contented housewife in her own kitchen.

When they had had their coffee and cheese sandwiches, she went to her coat on the chair, smiled happily, picked up the hidden bundle and said softly, "Look, Lou. You'll never guess what it is."

"What's that you've got there?"

"It's a present. You'll never guess."

"Who for?"

"For you, Lou."

"Gee whiz," he said. "Open it up and let me get my eye on it." He had been walking around the room in his shirt sleeves, with his new hard hat still on his head as though he were proud of it. With his hands on his hips, he stared at the parcel, watching her carefully lift a pale blue shirt out of the tissue paper, and a dark blue tie. "They'll look swell on you, kid," she said. "They'll look like a million dollars. Put them on now, baby, and let's have a look."

"Say, I have a mind to do that little thing," he said, holding the shirt and tie out at arm's length. "Blue always looks swell on me, don't it?" he said, walking across the room to the cracked looking-glass hanging on the wall. But as he began to unbutton the shirt he was wearing, he stopped suddenly, frowning, and said, "Where did you get the money for this stuff, Ronnie?"

"That priest gave me five dollars last night."

"That priest again, eh? What did he do? Come through?"

"No chance. He gave Midge five bucks and me five to help us out, I guess."

"I don't like the sound of this," Lou said. "I don't like it at all." His eyes looked very cold as he chewed his lips and thought, "What's the priest up to? What's he working at? You can't tell about priests. I don't trust priests. It's got to stop. He's soft-soaping her and he's talking business when he's laying coin on the line." Glaring at Ronnie, he said with a soft viciousness, "I told you, Ronnie, not to let the guy in, didn't I?"

"I know, Lou, but you can't raise a row and he was pretty decent, Lou."

"What's he mean to you, Ronnie?"

"He's nothing to me, he's nothing to you."

"See what I think of the pair of you. Take a look at this," he said, and he took the navy-blue tie that would have looked so splendid with the light blue shirt and began to tie it in knots, tearing it and jerking it, then throwing it savagely across the room. "I don't like him and I don't like you, see. I once knew a girl that got in dutch with a priest."

Shaking her head, Ronnie looked at the tie and looked at Lou. She felt so miserable she could not speak. With her head down, she went over to the bed and began to undress slowly, fumbling awkwardly with her dress. From her stocking, she took the three dollars she had earned that night and put it neatly on the bureau at the side of the bed. She got into bed without saying a word and turned her face to the wall.

Lou kept walking up and down, his feet thudding on all the creaking floor boards till he tired himself out. Then he looked at Ronnie's body huddled under the blankets and at the back of her neck; there was no movement, and while she lay like this he knew she was crying. Lou shook his head savagely from side to side. "Never mind, kiddo," he said at last. "Never mind, baby." He began to undress. Then he rolled her over roughly. "Here," he said. "Come on."

He held her angular body in his arms and kissed her, held her tight and made love to her and felt her holding him as if she would never let go, and he wanted to go on loving her all the time.

Five

THAT FIRST Friday in February, warm afternoon sunlight melted the snow on the street, and all day at the Cathedral the Blessed Sacrament, the body and blood of Christ, was exposed on the altar. People kept on entering the church in the afternoon for short visits. There was no crowd, people came singly, but they kept coming all day.

The Cathedral was an old, soot-covered, imitation Gothic church that never aroused the enthusiasm of a visitor to the city. It had been in that neighborhood for so long it now seemed just a part of an old city block. The parish was no longer a rich one. Wealthy families in fine old homes had moved away to new and more pretentious sections of the city, and poor foreigners kept coming in and turning the homes into rooming houses. These Europeans were usually Catholics, so the congregation at the Cathedral kept getting larger and poorer. Father Anglin really belonged to the finer, more prosperous days, and it made him sad to see how many of his own people had gone away, how small the collections were on Sunday and how few social organizations there were for the women. He was often bitter about the matter, although he should have seen that it was really a Protestant city, that all around his own Cathedral were handsome Protestant churches, which were crowded on Sunday with well-dressed people, and that the majority of the citizens could hardly have told a stranger where the Catholic Cathedral was.

On this first Friday of the month, when there was such a surprising amount of warm sunlight, people who went into the darkened church for a short visit blinked their eyes, kneeling, and did not see Father Dowling over to the left by the window. He was praying and contemplating the Blessed Sacrament. There was so much fervent earnestness in the way his hands were clasped and the way his head was bent and motionless, that he seemed to have become a part of the bench. No other priest spent so much time alone in the church on these Friday adorations as did Father Dowling. While a streak of sunlight filtered through the blue stained-glass window and shone on the back of his neck, he was meditating on love, on human love, divine love, and the love of man for God. Then he began to think of Ronnie and Midge, feeling that his love for them was growing, so that he might try and love them in his way as God must love everybody in the world. It seemed to him also that the more he could understand, love and help these girls, the closer he would be to understanding and loving God. So he made up his mind to be very patient, never to be angry if he was not immediately successful with them, and to see, if possible, that they were never in want. These thoughts filled him with hope.

As he left the church he decided to call that afternoon on Mr. James Robison, a wealthy lawyer, who had always been so willing to assist the priests in their charitable work, and ask him if he could get work for the girls.

So Father Dowling walked over to the lawyer's office, smiling, ruddy-faced, bowing to people he had never seen in his life before. He was looking forward eagerly to talking with Mr. Robison, because the lawyer was usually approached by Father Anglin when some favor was expected of him. Every time the young priest saw Mr. and Mrs. Robison coming out of the Cathedral on Sunday he felt a little glow of pride, knowing that no finer, more aristocratic, more devout people were coming out of church doors anywhere in the city. There had been a few occasions, too, when Mrs. Robison had invited Father

Dowling to their home on an evening for a game of bridge and, of course, he was always there when she permitted her home to be used for a tea for charity. Father Dowling often hoped the Robisons would not move out of the parish because he knew people in the neighborhood were in the habit of jeering and saying that all Catholics were poor, unsuccessful in business and socially unimportant. But they could never say that about the Robisons. Mr. Robison, a big, handsome, white-haired fellow with a florid face, was one of the few men in the city, who, on formal occasions, wore an opera cloak with a white silk lining. Father Dowling had seen him wearing this cloak with a high silk hat and silver-headed cane one night at a reception at the Bishop's palace. And besides, as a corporation lawyer, Mr. Robison knew the directors of the big trust companies, the bankers and politicians and the chief of police. He was a lawyer, and it was true there were many other lawyers, but he used to say often that he would never soil his hands by appearing in the police courts or having contact with the criminal element. He was a patron of music and he appeared with the socially prominent people of all denominations at the best concerts. He had perhaps only one weakness: if he gave a large amount to charity he expected his name to be put at the head of the list in the newspapers, but, after all, he was entitled to this primacy of position; the only doubtful consideration was whether he ought to insist upon knowing what other people were giving. But aside from these matters, when Father Dowling saw the lawyer and his two fine daughters come out of church after the eleven o'clock mass on Sundays and get into their car, while the liveried chauffeur held the door open and the poor people stood on the sidewalk with their mouths open, he rejoiced and wondered, for it seemed truly remarkable that a wealthy man could be such a Christian.

In the lawyer's office on the twentieth floor of an office tower, Father Dowling waited, sitting up straight, holding his black hat in both hands. The only thought worrying him was that Mr. Robison might have been displeased by some of his sermons attacking the materialism of the bourgeois world. There must have been some displeasure in the Robison home, Father Dowling knew, because for the last two weeks he had not been invited there in the evening for a cup of coffee and a game of bridge. Mrs. Robison had always pretended to admire his skill at cards.

But the lawyer this afternoon received him very heartily. "Come in, come in, Father," he shouted as soon as the office door was opened. "Sit right down. One moment. Here, have a cigar. Now, Father, what is it?"

Father Dowling, beaming and holding the cigar with great tenderness, said, "Beautiful weather out, simply wonderful. I've come to ask you a favor. Ah, Mr. Robison, we always seem to be asking favors of you. We're mendicants of the worst kind. Poor begging friars."

"That's quite all right. I'm the man to come to. I'd be disappointed if you went to any one else. How is Father Anglin's cold?"

"Much better. The bottle of whiskey you sent him was a great help."

"I hope you managed to get a nip?"

"Just a nip."

Father Dowling smiled warmly, thinking, "He's really a splendid Christian." His slight timidity left him. Clearing his throat, he leaned forward and said eagerly, "This is a simple matter, Mr. Robison. I'll put it very briefly. There are two girls in our parish in pretty desperate circumstances. They need work. I promised to get jobs for them. God knows what will happen if they don't get work." He was leaning forward over the desk, his blue eyes shining with sincerity and a conviction that he would not be denied. He looked very handsome. But Mr. Robison, regarding him with a blank expression and a complete lack of enthusiasm, tried to draw away by leaning further back in his chair and putting the tips of his fingers together, shutting Father Dowling out. "Does the man think I'm an employment agency in times like these, with the legal business on rock bottom, so many men out of work and half the city on civic relief?" he thought. Shaking his head sorrowfully, he said, "Ah, Father, these are difficult times for us all. I'd like to help you. I'll try to help you as a matter of fact. But if you must know the truth, I'm cutting my own staff. However, do I know the girls?"

"I don't think you do. I'm sure you don't."

"Old families in the parish, perhaps?"

"No, they are not well known. You might not know their names."

"Still, you'd give them a good recommendation, I suppose."

"I'm sure they'd be willing to work hard," Father Dowling said.

"It's a pity things are like this in these times. Many unfortunate people, even our own co-religionists, must suffer. The whole city is suffering. Men like myself must do all we can to keep the people contented and we're doing so. I don't mind saying, Father, that I can't agree with your social and political philosophy expressed in some of your sermons, but still, still . . ."

"You don't think you know any one who'd have work for the girls?" Father Dowling said so brokenly that the lawyer was startled.

"Say, it's not any relative of your own, is it, Father?" he said with more interest.

"No. Just two souls in our parish."

"Old friends of yours, maybe?"

"No, I haven't known them very long."

"I understand. I'll make a note of it. But I have next to no hope. I'll tell you what I'll do. I'll speak to my wife and ask her if she knows anybody who might want a couple of domestics. So don't worry, Father. It's mighty good of you to be taking such an interest in these people. Keep on with the good work. I admire your enthusiasm and energy."

Looking very upset, the young priest got up, his face beginning to flush with indignation. The lawyer was talking to him as though he were a child, a man so cloistered from life that he could not be expected to understand an economic depression, or the suffering of a city or a whole people – a cloistered young man, respected only because he was a priest. Father Dowling shook hands gravely with the lawyer, asked to be remembered respectfully to Mrs. Robison, and went out with his face burning.

As he walked along the crowded streets, with the women carrying parcels coming out of the big stores, he looked earnestly at each one as if he had never seen such people before. So many of them were well dressed, so many had their fur coats thrown open because of the sunlight, and were showing fine silk dresses. He longed to see Ronnie and Midge coming along the street in the crowd, well clothed, with some of the independence and contentment in their faces that he saw in the faces of these women. The snow was melting near the foundations of the buildings and the steam was rising. Father Dowling, standing by a drug store, kept thinking of the two girls with their old shoes and coats and their sewn-up stockings, in the hotel room, and he felt so much tenderness for them that he began to smile softly. As he heard the swishing of rubbers on the snow, he looked up and saw a beautiful woman with a mink wrap, fur-trimmed goloshes, and a face with a delicate hot-house bloom, getting into a big green car. Indignant, he wondered why God saw fit to permit so many people to have wealth and comfort, and so many to remain poor and hungry. "I'm sick and tired of those stupid platitudes about the poor," he thought. "A Christian is entitled to self-respect, to warmth and good clothing in any kind of decent society. Even a religious, who takes the vow of poverty in life, has everything he requires. He lacks nothing really. He has warmth and comfort and leisure. You can't be a Christian when you're hungry and have no place to sleep, for then you're hardly responsible for what you do." And the more he thought of social disorder, the more love and concern he felt for the two girls.

For the rest of the afternoon he went to see a few of his more wealthy parishioners. The women he called on welcomed him effusively, offered him wine or tea and talked to him as though he were a lovely boy, and he sat there very gravely, his eyes wandering around the room, his thoughts far away. And the more homes he visited the more he was convinced that moral independence and economic security seemed very closely related. He kept asking every one of these indulgent and respectful women if they would try and find employment for two girls of the parish. He pleaded with them, feeling that they were not taking him seriously, as they fawned over him, pampering him. The way some young women flirted with a priest disgusted him. Sometimes they even wrote letters to him, pretending to be making all kinds of revelations, when they were really shamelessly offering themselves to him without realizing how he might be tempted and tortured.

Six

FATHER Dowling had one young friend named Charlie Stewart, who had always been a great joy to him. He was a medical student, a thin man with a narrow face and sharp restless eyes, who had no religion, but who loved to discuss social problems. Father Dowling had met him at a meeting of a league for social reconstruction. At first Father Dowling had tried to get the young man to join the Church. In this he was not successful, so he had come to love him for his passion and the violence of his opinions. He used to irritate the young man by smiling and saying, "Ah, Charlie, you don't realize it, but all your intuitions are Catholic." He had dropped this kind of mockery only when Charlie began to insist he was thinking of joining the Communist party. It often puzzled Father Dowling to realize that Charlie, who had no faith and was a dreadful rationalist, had in many ways become his best friend. Of course, few people ever understood the terrible loneliness of a young parish priest, the dreadful necessity for him to have one friend to whose house he could go when he was tired and discouraged and take off his collar, stretch his legs, and relax and laugh like a human being. So many of the people who talked to the young priest with such stiff politeness would have been ill at ease if they could have seen him laughing, without his collar on. They preferred to leave him alone or treat him with distant respect.

As Father Dowling went along the street with his hat on

the back of his head at a ridiculous angle, he was thinking it was only the grace of God that had given him such a friend as Charlie Stewart. Night after night, sometimes till two o'clock in the morning, over many cups of coffee or a little beer, they had had fierce political arguments and gruelling philosophical discussions: they had talked of Karl Marx and the guilds of mediaeval times; they had spoken passionately about "beauty" in the abstract, and the general progress of the race toward the city of God. Father Dowling had got many themes for sermons out of these discussions.

Charlie Stewart's apartment was in a building overlooking a schoolyard. Charlie was in his shirt sleeves when Father Dowling came in, and his hair was hanging low over his thin, intellectual face. He took off his glasses and his eyes looked very red and tired. "Hello, Father. I was thinking about you yesterday," he said. "You haven't come to see me all week. Sit down. Take off your coat."

"I can't stay a minute," Father Dowling said anxiously. "I won't even sit down. I'm in a great hurry, Charlie." Father Dowling was twisting his hat nervously, looking very worried.

He was so quiet and ill at ease, so hesitant in his speech, that Charlie Stewart was silent, wondering what was the matter with him. The priest remained silent so long that Charlie imagined he was still offended over a discussion they had had the other night about celibacy. The priest had said that night, "I'm surprised a man of your intuitions can't appreciate the value of celibacy." And Charlie had jeered, "Faith, hope and celibacy, says St. Paul, and the greatest of these is celibacy."

"You don't look well to-night, Father. Have you been working hard? You look pale and worried," he said, and he thought, "What's bothering Father Dowling?"

"I've been feeling fine, Charlie."

"There's something agitating you, I can see that."

"I feel splendid. Listen, Charlie, this is very embarrassing. I'd mention it to no one but you. I need the loan of a little money. Have you got anything you can spare? Say fifteen dollars. Of course I'll square it off with you at the end of the month."

Charlie was surprised, but he said, "I'll show you what I've got." He took a small roll of bills out of his pocket. "I'm lucky to this extent. I just got money from my people. I can let you have twelve dollars. How's that?" As he offered the money, Father Dowling saw him frown slightly and look concerned, and he knew intuitively that Charlie was remembering he had a girl now whom he took out in the evenings. He was very much in love with this girl. That was one of the reasons why he and the priest had had fewer profound discussions during the last month.

Father Dowling felt humiliated to be taking this money. He drew in his breath, wetted his lips and looking very white-faced, he smiled and said, "God bless you, Charlie. God bless you. I'll say a little prayer for you as I go along the street."

"I want you to promise to meet my girl, Father."

"I will, Charlie. I'll like her, I know."

And when he was outside, walking rapidly with his head down, he was making a fervent little prayer. Some of the finest prayers he had ever made had been made sometimes when he was hurrying along the street. He prayed that Charlie Stewart might prosper because of his goodness. And he was thankful and proud that he had such a young friend. In all the city, he thought, no other priest had such an interesting friend, a man who was not only good-natured but full of his own wisdom, full of startling observation, speculative thought and, above all, a man with a simple heart.

He felt easier in his own mind. He took off his hat, wiped his perspiring forehead, and as he looked up eagerly at the stars he passed right by the Cathedral and kept on going around the block to the hotel.

Seven

FATHER Dowling went up the hotel stairs two steps at a time, rapped on the white door and waited, breathless, fearing no one would be in. But when the door was opened a few inches, Midge's round face peered out at him. She was puzzled. She hesitated almost as if she would close the door. It was time for her to go out. Her face had just been powdered carefully and her hair arranged and she was putting on her coat. She said doubtfully, "Were you coming in, Father?"

"Please, Midge," he said, and he went in as if the room were his own and he was relieved to be there. Twice he walked the length of the floor, wondering how he could explain that he had failed to find work for them and wondering, too, if his gift of a few dollars would seem too small after his promises. Midge was watching him so restlessly, and tapping her toe so impatiently that he felt unwelcome and said, "Were you planning to do anything?"

"Oh, no, Father," she said. "I was thinking maybe of going over to the store, but that doesn't matter at all."

"I thought we might talk a while," he said diffidently.

"I'm awfully glad to see you, Father," she said. "You know that. You know, we often talk about you now."

"That's splendid," he said, and he smiled with relief and began to take off his coat. His lips were moving faintly as if he were preparing certain arrangements of words. Sometimes he smiled a bit and hesitated, as if the thought behind the words amused him. And when she saw that he intended to stay for some time, she shrugged and pursed her mouth and curled up on the bed, her head supported by her hand and elbow. By this time she was at ease with the priest and watched him with curiosity. It was only when he looked at her steadily and simply with his very candid blue eyes that she felt uneasy. Father Dowling was so pleased to see her lying there, smiling, that he became almost inarticulate. "Do you know," he said suddenly, "you look now as if you would fit very easily into a decent home. That's the way I think of you. I pray that soon I shall see you in such a place. I was awfully glad to find you here when I called. That's the stuff. I'll soon be able to have the feeling that I'm calling here as I would on any other parishioner." He laughed apologetically. "Some of them are very strange people. They mightn't like you, but you mightn't like them, either. Oh well, that's not the way to speak of them. Underneath the surface many of them have splendid Christian characters."

"You're funny, Father. You think all people are nice, don't you?"

"Oh, no. To the contrary. I think many people are decidedly evil. It is sometimes necessary to pretend that they are nice. To make it more deplorable many are often evil of their own volition."

"What's volition?"

"Of their own free will. Because they want to."

"I'm glad you like me and Ronnie," she said. "I guess because we have plenty of volition, eh? Wait till I pull that on Ronnie. When she comes in I'll say, 'You've too much volition to-night,' and she'll think I'm insulting her."

"You two girls are very precious to me, almost more than the rest of my work," he said. "I want you to understand that. I think you do." He saw her relaxing; he felt her lazy good humor. It seemed to him that she ought to have a slow drawling charm. It seemed to him that already she had a little more contentment in her face and he really loved the way she was apt to burst out laughing, as if the faintest incident touched her deeply, as if the sensation of the most fleeting moment had to be savored fully. "That attitude in her is really Christian in the best sense of the word," he thought. "That desire to make each moment precious, to make the immediate eternal, or rather to see the eternal in the immediate."

And she was watching him lazily, thinking, "If he keeps on staying, I won't be able to go out. What does he want to say? There's something on his mind. He's a very nice man. Maybe I don't really want to go out. Maybe I could get him to come over here and sit beside me."

"Where's Ronnie?" he said at last. He had been trying not to seem worried. He had kept on pretending to himself that she would burst into the room in the way a girl comes rushing into the warmth from the cold night air. "Where's Ronnie?" he repeated. "Aren't you expecting her?"

"No. She's out with Lou."

"Who is Lou, Midge?"

"Lou's her fellow. She goes around with him."

"What kind of a fellow is he, a decent type, has he some character?"

"You'd better not take my word for it, Father. As far as I'm concerned he can go and jump in the lake. But then he doesn't like me."

"Is she in love with him?"

"She's nuts about him."

"Then I'd like to meet Lou some day."

"Don't worry, you will if you keep hanging around here."

"What time will she come?"

"Very late. Very, very late. You won't want to wait for her. You better forget about her for to-night."

Father Dowling rose and began to walk up and down the room. Several times he took out his watch, looked at it and sighed. He kept thinking he ought to go home, but then he would whisper to himself, "I'll wait twenty minutes more." He was almost afraid to go without seeing Ronnie, fearing that if he missed her he would lose track of her for a while and would not know what was happening to her. At last he stopped, smiled at Midge, took from his pocket an envelope containing the money he had borrowed, and with a strangely diffident apologetic nod, he slipped it under the cloth cover on the dresser. "I don't want you to have to worry about how you're going to live, do you see," he said.

Midge stiffened and craned her neck, longing to look in the envelope, but she held herself there, full of wonder at him, following him with her eyes as he went up and down the floor with the worried expression growing more severe. He kept taking out his watch. Finally he said, almost humbly, "Midge, would you do a small favor for me? Come around to the church some time. Just of an evening when the church is full. Will you do that?"

"I guess so," she said, looking upset and a bit resentful. He loved to have this response and see that indignant expression. It made him feel there was a depth to her that could be touched, some kind of feeling, even if only resentment, and he was much encouraged. "There's passion still there," he thought. "Just say you'll come," he said.

"All right, Father," she said awkwardly. "I'll do that for you. It won't cost me nothing, will it?"

"Bring Ronnie, too," he said.

He wanted to wait till Ronnie came in. The longer he waited the more he wondered where she was and what she was doing. He began to make uneasy, sporadic conversation with Midge, but whenever she began to get interested he would become thoughtful and silent. He saw that Midge was getting sleepy. Once he yawned himself. They both lay back and began to doze. Then Father Dowling sat up abruptly, saw Midge's eyes closed, saw how long her lashes were, and how her lips were parted and her breast was softly swelling, and he went out without disturbing her.

Eight

THE TWO girls often used to think that Father Dowling might actually be in love with them, he was so patient and tender. Sometimes he would pat one of them on the head, or hold out his hands to them. They used to try and sit on his knee or put their arms around him and looked puzzled when he pushed them away. They could not understand the nature of his feeling for them. They could not believe that sooner or later he would not want either one of them.

He met many of their friends, street girls, who came very late, regarded him with hostility and got used to him and talked as if he weren't there. There were two girls, Marge and Annie, who liked him and wanted to joke with him. Marge was a very heavy old blonde girl with wide hips and deep breasts and a loud, boisterous laugh that always startled him, and she used to say, "I'll bet you more men go to confession to me than to you. Sometimes you can't stop them telling the family dirt when they get into bed." Annie was a slender, hot-eyed, bad-tempered Mulatto. She tried many times to arouse Father Dowling and refused to accept his celibacy. One night, growing vicious, she stood in front of him and lifted her dark breast out of her dress and held it out to him, jeering and teasing. "Ain't that nice? Come on, change your luck, big boy," she said. The blood surged into his face, he looked uneasy, but he stood up and said, "You'll have to go, Annie. You should not have done that."

"You liked it, you know you liked it."

"You must never do anything like that again, do you hear?"

"Leave him alone, Annie," Midge said jealously. "Did no one ever turn you down before? You've been turned down by everybody in this burg that wears pants."

Father Dowling had a man's passion, and as he sat there looking furtively at the dark girl, and at Midge and Ronnie, he suddenly saw them just as young women, making him full of longing as they used to do when he was a boy. He wanted to take their soft bodies and hold them while his arms trembled. He wanted to put his head down on white warm softness. The blood seemed to be swelling into his loins. Their laughter, their bawdily relaxed bodies which he saw now magnified by his longing into loveliness, brought a tension into his own limbs which he could not break. But then his forehead began to perspire, his whole body relaxed and he trembled and felt ashamed. "I ought not to be ashamed of being tempted," he thought. "I am not a eunuch. The Church will not accept a eunuch for a priest. I'm a normal man and I wouldn't be normal if I wasn't tempted. But I'll never be tempted like this again."

There were other nights when he dreamed and woke up feeling wretched, almost willing to decide not to go to the hotel again. But he always realized that to stay away for such a reason would be an act of weakness and lack of faith. Therefore, he remained patient and friendly with all these girls till they all got used to him. They began to ask his advice on many matters. They had more problems than he had ever heard in the confessional. They used to like the way he reasoned with them considerately.

Lou would never believe Ronnie when she insisted that the priest was not getting something from the girls. He used to jeer and tell stories about tunnels that ran underground from monasteries to convents, and he hoped to come into the room some time and embarrass Father Dowling, whom he had never really met.

One night Lou came in when the priest was there, but he walked past him, with his derby hat far over on one side of his head, as if he had not seen him and stood idly at the window, whistling through his teeth and sometimes snapping his fingers. Father Dowling, who had not taken off his coat because he had come in a great hurry, sat in the chair regarding Lou shrewdly. Lou turned, stared at the priest's spotless, shining white collar and smiled sarcastically. Father Dowling smiled, too, so that the skin around his eyes was all wrinkled up, and Lou did not know what to say.

"This is Lou. You've heard me speak of Lou, my fellow," Ronnie said. Looking at Lou, she pleaded with her eyes as she scraped her foot in a small circle on the carpet. Father Dowling got up and put out his hand with so much heartiness that Lou was surprised into shaking hands limply. The mildness in the priest's eyes and yet the strength in his big hands disturbed Lou. Lou respected strength. Father Dowling said, "I've heard all about you, Lou. You've got a splendid girl in Ronnie. Be good to her, eh? A man would never want a better girl."

"Oh, I treat her pretty good as it is," Lou said. "Of course, I don't give her jewels and take her horseback riding, but I always give her what I call a good break."

"I'm glad to hear it. You're a good fellow, we'll be friends, I know."

"All right with me," Lou said. Then he added awkwardly, making a sharp swoop with his left hand, "But I don't want you interfering between me and the girl, see."

"Of course not. I'm glad to hear you speak like that. Lots of fine manly fibre, eh? We'll see more of each other."

As the priest turned to pick up his hat, Lou wanted to insult him. But Father Dowling had so much assurance, such an imperturbable smile that Lou felt it necessary to be careful. At last he blurted out the words he had been wanting to say. "How long have you been here with Ronnie?"

"About twenty minutes. Why?" Father Dowling asked.

Lou tried desperately to say, "Well, you're going to pay her something, aren't you? What do you think she does for a living?" but he faltered, his face reddened. "I was glad to meet you. That's all, Father."

"There wasn't something else you wanted to say?"

"That's all."

As Father Dowling went out he was thinking, "Lou's a bad actor, a bad character, I can see that." But he felt, too, that Ronnie loved Lou, and he did not want to say anything to him in front of her that might hurt her.

Nine

THE TIME when Father Dowling went to meet Charlie Stewart's girl, he found that as soon as he got to the apartment house by the schoolyard he had become shy. As he looked up at the lighted apartment window and saw the shadow of a woman moving on the shade he remembered how he had at first been angry because a woman had become important in his young friend's life. Now he knew he had dreaded to meet the girl. Walking away a little piece, he turned around and saw her form again passing the lighted window. In his own celibate life he had always been content, but now he wondered if that contentment had made him dry and wooden, so he could not understand Charlie's longing for happiness with this girl. She was a Catholic. Perhaps it was his duty, he thought suddenly, to go in and tell her that she ought not to marry a man like Charlie who was without faith, no matter how much he loved her. But supposing he went in there and saw that they were both very much in love. "Perhaps through her influence Charlie might learn to think differently," he thought.

As he looked up at the lighted window, he was afraid it might be better to try and understand the happiness the young man and girl might be seeking so eagerly before he spoke against their marriage. "I won't say anything to her to-night," he thought. This was a compromise. He excused himself because he knew the girl would look at him shrewdly, maybe with dislike, and remember that he had advised Charlie not to marry her. In going in to meet them, when they loved each other in a way that he could not comprehend, because for him their marriage could hardly be sanctioned, he felt he might be going where he had no right to go. He felt the girl might look at him and hate him. "I'll go in very cheerfully and pretend I've never thought about the matter at all," he said.

But when Father Dowling was in the apartment, shaking hands, with his face red and smiling, the girl, Pauline, who understood so well why Father Dowling did not want the marriage, smiled at him warmly as if she had been wanting to meet him for a long time; she could not believe from what she had heard about him that he would say Charlie ought not to marry her. She was a very tall, fair girl with an elegant manner, who wore fine expensive clothes.

Charlie was talking to her now as if Father Dowling was not a priest but an old friend, and she kept turning her head and looking at the priest's embarrassed face, hardly able to conceal a slight amusement. But as soon as Father Dowling looked at the girl's blue eyes and saw her smile suddenly, he knew she had wondered maybe many nights whether she could get a priest to marry her to Charlie.

As the priest sat opposite the two of them the girl's face was radiant. They both seemed very much in love, and she said, "I've heard so much about you, Father. Charlie keeps saying he wants you to marry us." The priest liked her and couldn't help thinking she would make a fine wife. "If she's a good Catholic, and if Charlie's intuitions are so often traditionally Catholic, even if he thinks he's Communistic, maybe it's in the hands of God whether he has faith or not. Faith is the gift of God. It is in God's hands, especially if they are determined to marry," and after this thought he smiled as though he had suddenly freed himself of the problem.

"I've heard so much about your conversation. I'd just love to listen to the two of you talking," she said.

"No, not to-night," he said. "I'm happy to be here with you and Charlie. I know you'll make him a splendid wife." He blushed, remembering that the last argument had been about celibacy, and Charlie had yelled, "Faith, hope and celibacy, and the greatest of these is celibacy, says St. Paul." He nodded his head with the diffidence of a man who feels he may be intruding, but who wants to stay. "I'd be very happy to-night if we didn't become intellectual, but if you'd just let me sit here and listen, and maybe you'd talk about your plans or what you've been doing and where you've been going, and perhaps what you expect to do when you get married."

The medical student started to talk solemnly about his plans for the future; he was going away to another city. His thin, clever face lit up as he told how he wanted to specialize in nervous diseases: he would like to go to Vienna, he said, and study in the hospitals there. When he paused, the tall girl who had been listening intently, with her head leaning forward, her face full of sincerity, began to speak rapidly, carrying on just from the point where Charlie had left off, making more plans, telling how they would go to Vienna because they both were saving their money. When she, too, had to stop to get her breath, Charlie went on slowly, explaining that he loved and respected his work, and wanted to keep growing into it, that he would work like a dog and still remain very willing. "Pauline understands the situation perfectly," he said. "We know just what we want to do. The whole thing is there before us if we'll only do it," and they smiled confidently, as if their souls remained open to each other. Father Dowling, watching and listening, did not know why he felt so joyful at one moment, so inexpressibly sad at another. It filled him with joy to be there, close to these two young people who were so much in love, and yet it was a kind of love he would never be able to realize completely, although he assured himself it was just a part of a greater, more comprehensive love that he often felt very deeply. In a moment of wistfulness, he rubbed his plump hand nervously over his face, listening like a child, but he was thinking that this beautiful girl who was so well dressed lived comfortably, while the two girls who most concerned him in the world, and who were now his special care, looked shabby, lived in mean rooms and probably were often hungry.

The student and his girl were still talking, having almost forgotten that he was there. He stole a nervous glance at Pauline's fine kid shoes, at her black crêpe dress, so rich-looking and probably so expensive, and then, with the color mounting in his smooth cheeks, he glanced quickly at her legs in the sheerest of fine crêpe hose. Sighing, he leaned back and closed his eyes. But they did not notice him. At that moment he was feeling more love for the two girls than he had ever felt before because their lives were so wretched, because their clothes were so shabby, and even when they bought new things they were in poor taste. "Midge bought a new hat but it did not really look like this girl's hat," he thought. Suddenly Father Dowling was full of such eagerness that he leaned forward, waiting for Charlie to stop talking. He was moistening his lips, smiling, hardly hearing the conversation at all. "I wonder," he said. "I wonder if you would do something for me, Pauline?"

"I'd do anything I could, Father."

"I'm sure you would, but I don't want to impose on you."

"I won't let you do that, Father. I'm pretty ruthless."

"This is a matter that would only take up a little of your time. It's like this. I know two girls, sort of nieces, not in very good circumstances. I was wanting them to have new clothes for the spring. . . ."

"Go on, Father."

"That's where you come in."

"You want me to help you with the clothes."

"Well, as you can see, I can't very well go and buy them clothes. I'd have no skill in such matters. Besides, they mightn't want to wear what I'd buy. If you would do this for me . . . ." He began to look terribly embarrassed. He felt his face getting hot while they smiled broadly, and then he, too, began to laugh with great heartiness, his face all red and full of open enthusiasm now, and when he got his breath at last, he said, "It no doubt must seem a bit funny to take advantage of you immediately in this way, Pauline, but that's the kind of person I am. Ask Charlie. I've been taking advantage of him ever since I've known him."

"I don't believe it, Father," she said. "I'd be glad to help you if you'd just tell me what sort of thing, what kind of dress, how much you want to pay and so on. Just give me something to go on. What are the girls like?"

"One of them is about your height and she's fair, too. Her feet look to me to be about your size. Let's say that for her. You get something like you'd get for yourself. Shoes, stockings, and dress. What do you think?"

"You've no idea what color for the dress?"

"I think that black dress you've got on looks beautiful on you," he said honestly. "I like that bit of white at the neck, too."

"That's fine. I didn't think you had noticed it. What's the other girl like?"

"She's different. Her feet are smaller for one thing. They are very tiny little feet. I'd say a size and a half smaller than yours. And she's a good four inches shorter. But mind, she is of a normal build, not fat or awkward nor thin either. And she's dark with brown eyes. What do you think would look good on her?"

"Gray is being worn a lot now, gray with gray shoes and gray stockings. A gray outfit."

"Lovely," he said. "Simply splendid."

"Do you want to pay much?"

"I don't want it to be cheap stuff, but not expensive of course. Maybe if you'd look around you'd get a bargain. Then send it up to me and I'll pay for it."

"I'll be downtown to-morrow. I'll look around in the morning maybe. How's that?"

"God bless you," he said. "If I were a young fellow I'd have a girl like you."

His own thoughts were now so delightful that he got up to go, so he could enjoy them undisturbed. They coaxed him to stay; he pleaded he had work to do. They were both smiling at him warmly, and when he went out to the street his first thought was, "What a remarkable quality that girl has. What a pity they aren't both more devout Christians. Charlie's in the Church in heart and he doesn't really know it." Then he walked on, still smiling, till he remembered he had said Ronnie and Midge were nieces of his. "That was a lie," he thought and he was immediately bothered, walking along, staring at the sidewalk. "Of course, I couldn't have explained who they actually were. But I don't want to get into the habit of lying about them. That's inexcusable." And while he wanted to let his thoughts leap forward with pleasure to images of the girls in new clothes, he resolutely forced himself to go on considering the danger of petty lying.

Ten

THE AFTERNOON the boxes containing the dresses came to the priest's house, Father Dowling was waiting and he wrote out a check for sixty-five dollars for the delivery man. The housekeeper, old Mrs. Arrigo, who had called him to the door, looked with curiosity at the bundles and smiled up at him, for she liked him more than any of the other priests. She was a little, fat, gray-haired, Italian woman, who always smiled and was very pious. "Can't I help you with those boxes, Father?"

"Oh no," he said anxiously. "I'll look after them myself, thank you."

After carrying the boxes upstairs to his bedroom he looked at them for a long time, full of eagerness, but knowing really that he would not permit himself to open these boxes of young women's clothing in the house. They must remain there on his bed till he took them away early in the evening. Furthermore, he would not permit himself to indulge in too much anticipation, either, of the pleasure that would be his when he saw the startled surprise on the girls' faces. All these thoughts and resolutions occurred to him as reasons why he should not want to open the boxes there in the room, when some one was apt to come upstairs and see him, or call him, and force him to make very embarrassing explanations. The other young priest in the house, Father Jolly, knew that he had no nieces. Besides, there was always a kind of good-natured malice between

Father Dowling and Father Jolly. It had begun when Father Dowling had wanted the other young priest's room because it had a set of bookshelves and his own had none. Father Jolly had immediately decided to go in for literature himself, and he would read Tolstoy, or Conrad, or anybody else that Father Dowling recommended and come back in a few days, drink two or three bottles of beer, and say, "My, isn't that author carnal? Do you really like him?" and at the dinner table, with old Father Anglin turning down his lip contemptuously, he would force Father Dowling to defend a carnality in Tolstoy that didn't really exist. Sometimes these arguments about literature became so impassioned that old Father Anglin was drawn into them and he gave it as his opinion that all art, being sensual, tended to detract from man's one primal instinct, his need of the faith and his desire to worship God. Father Jolly, his head bobbing up and down enthusiastically, readily agreed with the old priest. But he kept his room with the bookshelves, teased Father Dowling, accused him of scheming to get it, gave up his interest in literature unless the books were on the Cardinal's white list, and remained gravely suspicious of Father Dowling's respect for modern carnal authors. If Father Jolly saw these boxes he would at once associate them with unorthodox notions. "Ah, I must not have such thoughts," Father Dowling said to himself, going out of the room.

In the evening, almost as soon as it was dark enough so that he thought he would not be noticed, Father Dowling took his two boxes and the smaller bundle and set out for the hotel on the other side of the block. It was a clear mild evening. The snow had nearly all gone from the streets. There was a freshness in the air that made him think of approaching spring. He passed a young man and a girl walking very close together and the girl's face was so full of eagerness and love Father Dowling smiled. As soon as the mild weather came the young people began to walk slowly around the Cathedral in the early evening, laughing out loud or whispering and never noticing anybody who smiled at them. The next time Father Dowling, walking slowly, passed two young people, he smiled openly, they looked at him in surprise and the young man touched his hat with respect. Father Dowling felt suddenly that he loved the whole neighborhood, all the murmuring city noises, the street cries of newsboys, the purring of automobiles and rumble of heavy vehicles, the thousand separate sounds of everlasting motion, the low, steady and mysterious hum that was always in the air, the lights in windows, doors opening, rows of street lights and fiery flash of signs, the cry of night birds darting around the Cathedral and the soft low laugh of lovers strolling in the side streets on the first spring nights. He felt he would rather be here in the city and at the Cathedral than any place else on earth, for here was his own home in the midst of his own people.

Closer to the hotel, he felt a deep amusement within him, as if he could feel in advance the astonishment that would be in the girls' eyes. The bundle, though not heavy in his arms, was very awkward to carry, and as he shifted it from one arm to the other, he could already see himself standing in the hotel room, peering into the boxes, more eager than the girls to see what they contained.

But when he entered the hotel and rapped on the door there was no answer. Leaning against the wall, listening, he heard no sound and then he walked downstairs slowly, his feet heavy on each step and a fear in him that he might go many times up the stair to that white door and knock and there never would be an answer. The silence that follows an eager knock on a door can be a dreadful thing, he thought. Many times he had gone upstairs with like eagerness and always deeply buried within him was the same fear that they would not be there. Yet they were nearly always there, or they came shortly afterwards.

He was standing by the hotel door holding his boxes tightly when the man at the desk called out ingratiatingly. "Are you looking for your girl friends, mister? They'll be along shortly, I think."

"Thank you," Father Dowling said. His hand wanted to go creeping up to his collar to make sure it was covered, then he reflected with relief that the man had called him "Mister." Mr. Baer, who was sitting at the desk with the most benevolent, considerate smile on his round face, a smile that included comprehendingly all the desires of the world and their satisfactions, was tapping the tips of his fingers together, anxious to begin a conversation. But Father Dowling stepped out to the street thinking, "I decidedly don't like that man."

Up and down the street he went, feeling sure he would not see the girls that evening. At last he saw them coming, crossing the road, hesitating because of the passing automobiles, holding on to each other's arm; he heard a ripple of loud laughter, and they started to run a little before they saw him at all.

"Just a minute, Midge. Just a minute, both of you," he called out.

"Look, Ronnie, it's Father," Midge said.

"Wouldn't that knock you cold. Just when we were talking about him, and he pops up here."

"We've been loafing around window shopping. Isn't it cockeyed? There we were gaping in a window talking about you and here you were looking for us."

"I came about twenty minutes ago. If you hadn't come now I would have gone looking for you."

"Look at the parcels Father's carrying, Midge. What's in them? Were you going some place?"

"I'll show you what's in them. That's exactly what I want to do. Could I go in with you?"

As he followed the girls upstairs he tried to keep a severe, stern expression on his face so the man at the desk dare not smile, but he was really so eager to show his gifts that the corners of his mouth kept twitching into faint smiles of amusement. In the bedroom he put the bundles on the floor and sat down with his blue eyes shining bright. "Open them, both of you," he said. And he leaned back, relaxing and feeling a marvellous contentment while they knelt down on the floor, their heads together, their faces so serious, pulling at the paper, snapping off the string, pulling the lids off the boxes, holding up a black crêpe dress, then pulling out the gray dress. And then he could resist no longer, he leaned forward, peering eagerly over Ronnie's shoulder at the dresses he had not seen. "The gray one, the gray stockings and the gray shoes are for you, Midge, and the black dress and shoes are for you, Ronnie."

Still crouched on the floor, the two girls were silent, then Ronnie, rolling her eyes and lifting her head up to him, whistled softly. Midge just kept on staring at Ronnie.

"I wonder if you might put them on now and let me see you," he said mildly. "Just before I go. I must hurry to-night."

"Oh, Father, you're a peach, honest to God you are."

"I'd love to do something for you, Father. Isn't there something you'd want me to do? Let me kiss you."

"Oh no, don't do that," he said quickly.

"It wouldn't hurt just once. Do you think it might give you the jitters?"

"No. Not that. You can be good to me just by thinking of me sometimes and being a good girl and feeling you've nothing to worry about. See."

Then the girls picked up the dresses and went silently into the other room, and for a long time Father Dowling waited, glancing impatiently at the door every time he heard a sound. Closing his eyes, he kept on waiting with a strange breathlessness, as if some transformation in the girls, far deeper than a mere change of clothing, would be effected there before his eyes.

And when they returned, shyly standing in front of him and looking around with an awkward uncertainty, glancing one at the other in a curious mutual uneasiness, he said nothing, he watched in silence and he did not even smile. Then they smiled timidly. They couldn't get rid of their feeling of shyness, they tried laughing at each other. "Look at you, Midge," Ronnie said. "Look at yourself," Midge said. Midge looked almost dainty in the gray dress, with her face paler and her eyes round with endless surprise. In the black crêpe dress with the long, severe, but graceful lines, some of the awkwardness seemed to have gone out of Ronnie, and her hair looked fairer, her face fresher. With this new timidity, lasting for just a few moments, she seemed severely honest, severely forthright in appearance.

"My goodness, I'm astonished at both of you. I don't know what to say," Father Dowling said.

"Do we look elegant?" Midge asked.

"You look – well, you look natural, as you should always look, and rather charming, both of you. You take my breath away."

So they felt easier in their thoughts. They began to laugh and walk around gaily, Midge extending her left hand gracefully to Ronnie and making a little curtsy. Then they both laughed again with a fine free happiness; they shrugged their shoulders, they became simply themselves, and while still looking pleased, they turned good-naturedly to the priest.

"Ah, you know somebody, Father, who likes nice clothes," Midge said. "Now who would it be? Have you a little lady tucked away some place?"

"I'll bet you've had a girl all the time," Ronnie said.

"Don't say things like that," he said softly.

"I'm only trying to kid you. You're a prince. I never met anybody so kind."

"Why do you do all these crazy things for us, Father?" Midge asked.

"You know why. Because I care for you and sometimes worry about you and hope so much that you'll keep trying to forget this room and all the people that ever came here. And all the nights you ever wandered around. That would satisfy me."

But he did not notice that they had become uneasy while he was speaking. He remained motionless, his young, smooth face very calm and a peculiar, wondering, remote expression in his eyes. He was not hearing anything they were saying to him. He was remembering how they had seemed so shy, with a kind of naïve, awkward innocence, when they returned to the room in the new clothes, and it seemed wonderful to him that he had discovered these traits in them. Nothing they could have said by way of thanking him could have repaid him as they had done already without knowing it. He felt very happy to have thought of the dresses. It seemed that for a long time he had been groping and scraping away at old reluctant surfaces and suddenly there was a yielding life, there was a quickening response. He sat there hardly smiling, looking very peaceful.

Eleven

IN A LITTLE upstairs Chinese restaurant in the early spring evening, Ronnie, Midge and Lou were having a sandwich and a cup of coffee. They were sitting by the window and could see the street below, see the crowds moving slowly under the brilliant electric lights and the women on the pavements who had discarded their fur coats now and had on brightly colored cloth coats for spring and Easter time. Midge was wearing her gray dress and gray shoes and Ronnie, too, had on the black dress the priest had given her. But the girls to-night were meditative and solemn. Even Lou was worried. On Midge's small round face there was a look of dreadful uneasiness, and a scared trembling inside her that did not show itself because she never moved, nor smiled, nor spoke. Even her head was held rigid and motionless. Her eyes looked too brilliant and her face was a little thinner now than it had been two weeks ago. Every few moments, she stared wonderingly at Ronnie, begging her to say something comforting or something that would make her laugh and forget why the three of them were having such a solemn conference.

"Never mind, kiddo. It's really nothing," Ronnie said. "It's just a matter of a little while and then you're right back again fresh as a daisy. I know."

"If you take my advice," Lou said, leaning over the table and patting Midge's hand, "you'll go to a hospital and take the treatments and make it all in a day's work. Don't you see, kiddo?"

"Do you hear what Lou's saying, kid? Lou knows."

"I'm just giving you the straight dope, cold, and not trying to soften it up," Lou said.

"I guess that's what I'd better do," Midge said. She tried to smile. She tried to feel reasonable, but the mounting dread within her was terrifying her as though she were a frightened little girl. She began to look at both of them helplessly.

"Will they hurt me?" she asked.

"Lou says it's nothing. It's just like having a cold, Midge."

"It used to be something to really worry about," Lou said. "But that was years ago. But it's nothing now, baby."

"I told you Lou would say that, Midge. It's nothing at all now," Ronnie said.

But Midge was so gloomy that Ronnie began to try and amuse her in many little ways. She folded her hands piously across her chest. "Ah, poor child, it's a great pity. Now if you'd just say a little prayer. If you would just think of me occasionally."

Midge smiled slightly. They had often mocked the priest in this way. Ronnie went on eagerly, "Won't you come and see me some time, child?"

"Yes, Father," Midge said, nodding her head and turning her eyes up angelically.

"Have you been baptized, child?"

"Ah, yes, indeed, Father. Three or four times, once last night and once the night before. And when I get some money I'm going to get drunk some more."

"Ah, but they are not good baptisms, my girl. Was the thing done properly?"

"As well as they could do it, Father. I am a small girl and you ought not to expect too much of me."

"If you would not try so hard, but just listen to the dictates of your heart."

"I have listened, Father."

"And what did you hear, child?"

"I heard the footsteps of my lord."

"And were they coming closer?"

"Oh yes, Father, closer and closer."

"And then what did you do, child?"

"I said the old man's coming and if I'm caught like this with my skirts up it'll look like a hard winter, I mean a cold winter, Father." With her head tilted to one side, Midge was making silly faces she thought appropriate to a pious woman, and then both girls began to snicker, and Lou let out a deep roaring laugh. "That's swell," he said. "You ought to team up and go into vaudeville. Keep on. Give us some more. The poor old duffer. Drag me in on this some way, won't you? I ought to be able to get my finger in for something, don't you think, kid? I've got a good heart, too, don't you think, Ronnie?"

But Midge, looking at him vacantly for a moment said irritably, "Let's get out of here in a hurry. I get fed up on the stuff," and they got up and left the restaurant. As soon as they were in the street, walking slowly up among the crowd that was enjoying the mildness of the first spring evenings, the last bit of eagerness for mockery of the priest went out of Midge. She heard Lou still trying to continue the conversation and the laughter about the priest; she heard Ronnie replying rapidly, saw her leaning on Lou's arm in her eagerness to hear more of his wit that kept them both laughing, and while Midge walked on and heard these sounds, on these streets where she had walked so often, in the neighborhood where she wandered every evening, she felt she could hardly drag herself along. She was looking straight ahead, but she kept seeing a long row of impenetrable faces. Sometimes she tried to remember and study these faces as if she might pick out and remember the one that was the cause of her sickness now. Her body began to feel so heavy and tired that she did not want to see anything, she did not even want to see the row of bright windows, the rooming houses, or the Cathedral on the corner; she longed to be able to close her eyes tight so she would not keep seeing hundreds of brutal faces and groping for one among them. "What will become of me? What can I do? Who will look after me? Who will pay the bills? Who will keep me?" she kept asking herself. "Maybe if I had got a job a few months ago it would not be like this now, but there was no job. There was nothing. There is nothing really now. No one's walking beside me, there's no street, no sound, there's nothing." And there seemed to be only darkness and numbness within her and all around her. Out of this darkness came a flicker of life, first a hatred for every one she had taken to the hotel, and then a breathless hope that she would go out that evening and find someone who would want her, who would go away content and then later begin to dread that night and be full of hate for her. But the resentment was so strong in her it could not last. She grew full of fear, dreadfully scared of the mockery she had been making with Ronnie a few minutes ago. "I didn't mean anything, God. If I only could get better, if I only would be all right afterwards, I'd go away, maybe back to Montreal and live at home. I've always really believed in you, God. I'm just scared now, that's all. Just don't be too hard on me, God." And as she kept on walking beside Ronnie and Lou, quite clearly she heard them laughing, she felt the night air, she saw the streets again.

In the hotel, when they had thrown off their coats, the three of them were dispirited for a moment, though Lou was still determined to go on burlesquing the priest. This kind of mockery made him very jolly. As he stood in the middle of the floor looking around for something he might use as a stage prop, he grinned and practised raising his heavy eyebrows, shooting them up high on his forehead, then lowering them and bowing his head slightly. He wanted to find something in the room that would look like a Roman collar, but nothing attracted him. In the end he took out his handkerchief, tied it around his neck and looking very much like a gunman he went to the door and pretended to be coming into the room. In a deep, hollow voice, he said, "Am I disturbing you, girls? Go right ahead with whatever you're doing. I'll just sit here and take it all in. I've got my eye on one of you little sisters, but I'm not telling you which one it is. That's a surprise I'm keeping till I get her alone. Let us pray."

"You don't look like Father Dowling at all, Lou," Ronnie said.

"What do I look like? Take a good look at me."

"You look like you might be going to hold up a bank."

"I thought I looked as if I might be going to lift up a skirt."

As soon as she heard Father Dowling's name, Midge wished he would come that night to see them, and she was not wishing now out of any regret for mockery, or feeling of uneasiness, but it seemed to her that neither Lou nor Ronnie, nor anybody else but him in the city could understand the way she was feeling.

"Does Lou seem to you to be very funny to-night?" she asked Ronnie. "He's a cute fellow always, I know, but does he seem funny to you?"

"What's the matter with him, Midge? Why have you got your knife in Lou?"

"I'm sick sitting here listening to him. Why don't you tell him to take a run around the block?"

"You know what's the matter with that dame," Lou said. "She's worried. Count out anything she says. Anyway, who the hell's this Father Dowling? What do you think he's after? What's there in it for him? The trouble with Midge is she just wants to play him herself."

"You're crazy, Lou. She never asks him for no more than he gives me."

"How do you know what she's getting out of him? Is she telling you? I don't trust that dame."

"If you don't get out of here, Lou, I'll throw that bottle at you," Midge said. "I'm sick listening to you. You come hanging around here cutting in on every penny Ronnie makes and God knows what for. I could never see you for trees. Now get out of here quick."

But Lou walked over slowly and stood beside her, thinking of beating her as he had once beaten her before when she had caused trouble between him and Ronnie. "I'll smack you, sister. I'll smack you down and give you plenty," he said solemnly. But Ronnie grabbed hold of him by the arm and said, "Please, Lou, go on out. Do it for me. Can't you see she's feeling bad and things look blue for the poor kid. Go on, honey. She's feeling like a nut now."

Lou glowered at both of them, then he turned, and, with a lofty contempt for women, he picked up his hat and coat and rushed out without putting them on.

And Ronnie sat down beside Midge and said, "Gee, kid, I wish you wouldn't try and get Lou sore on me. I don't know what I'd do without Lou. I don't want ever to be without him. See, baby?"

"I didn't want to cause any trouble, Ronnie."

"I know. I know the way you're feeling. You ain't no trouble."

"You know the way I'm feeling? I don't know as you do. To-day I read my teacup. I saw a ship, or it might have been a tombstone."

"Aren't you sure it was a ship?"

"I say it might have been a ship but I thought it was a tombstone and that means I'm going to die."

"How do you know you're going to die? You can't believe in teacups, not in all you see in teacups, but if it was me . . ."

"If it was you . . ."

"I'd say, what's the difference, kiddo. Supposing you die, where are you? And supposing you live, where are you? And you can't always go by teacups."

"That's why I say it might have been a ship. Is that some one at the door?"

"Some one's tapping on the door."

"Sh, sh, sh, I'll die if I see a soul. I don't want to see a soul."

"Maybe it's Lou," Ronnie said.

"It can't be Lou. I know Lou and you know Lou, he'd come right in. Maybe it's the priest."

"It might be the priest."

"Then he'll come back. I know the priest."

"There he goes. I can hear him on the stair."

"I'm glad he's gone. I want to be alone. I'd like to sit and figure it out. It might have been a ship, but it looked like a tombstone. Sit down, Ronnie, and don't keep listening. Talk and talk and talk to me."

Twelve

LOU LEFT the hotel, walking slowly, with his head down, and even if he had to walk all night, he intended to think through the problem clearly. For days he had felt the simplicity, comfort and security of his life being menaced. There had been for a long time a fine orderliness about his life that made him feel honest and almost respectable. As he shuffled along slowly, he couldn't figure out why the priest wanted to disturb a life that had become so pleasant. He felt uneasily that he might lose Ronnie; to-night in the hotel there had been a quarrel about the priest. "I'd like to wring Midge's neck," he thought. "I never did like her. She's a little snip."

Lou had never felt so insulted and injured; he longed to go home and talk to his mother and sister, only he felt sure they would look at him dumbly with silent, white faces. The last time he had gone home his mother, a little woman, who was too old to work, had screamed, "You're no son of mine. Lord help me. You're a rebuke from God for some sin of my youth. Get out of here, you scamp." Then his thin-faced sister, Gertie, had tried to push him out of the house and he had found it necessary to take hold of her by the neck till she had struggled and panted and in a weak whisper promised to keep her hands off him. Of course, Lou knew his family really loved him. Even on that night, after the shouting and pushing, he had stayed with them for two or three hours, patting his mother's back and kissing her; and he had put his arms around Gertie, too, and finally, after he had talked persuasively a long time, they had begun to understand that it was difficult in these hard times for a young man to find steady employment. They had begun to speak tenderly; they had wanted to loan him money. His mother, breathing hard and saying, "Dear, oh dear, where did I put it?" had hunted all over the house for her purse, and Gertie had run upstairs and come down eagerly with a smile and a two-dollar bill.

But Lou knew that if he went home now, they would try again to keep him out of the house. Instead of thinking about his family, he began to remember with a wonder and tenderness the first time he had ever met Ronnie. Two years ago it was; a pal of his, phoning him at three o'clock in the morning, had got him out of bed and the friend had said he was at a party, where there was a girl who felt sure she would like Lou just from hearing them all talking about him. "I've been telling her about you, Lou. She wants a fellow and she thinks you sound mighty fine. She wants a fellow with class and plenty of nerve." Lou had got dressed and had gone to the party and had met Ronnie. Lou was not surprised to learn that the girl had heard so many fine stories about him; he was really astonished to find that he liked her so very much.

"We just seemed to be thrown together by what you might call fate. Just like two peas in a pod," he thought. "So I'm not going to stand for anybody cutting in." Walking with his shoulders held so that his whole body was leaning back, he felt like a strong, powerful man. Though he stared defiantly at anybody who noticed him, he remained puzzled and worried. Never in his life had he felt so indignant, and there was such strength within him that he forgot he was a little fellow, and said, "I'll see this thing right through, myself."

When he crossed the road at the corner, heading for the club over the restaurant, the light shone on his sober, worried face and threw a long shadow of him on the road, with one hand in his pocket, his narrow shoulders still thrust back.

In the poolroom he went from one table to another, staring at the green surfaces of the tables under the pyramids of white light, grinning at friends, passing on restlessly till at last he sat down all alone on the bench by the wall. He hardly looked up even when some one spoke to him. Here he was a man whom everybody respected. He never asked assistance; no one was a better pool player; he was never in trouble with the police; he was a little man, but very tough and afraid of nobody, who sat there facing a problem as if he knew the high regard his friends had for him, and it was an obligation to preserve this respect. A big man in a peak cap, Red Hertz, an old friend with two or three women on a string, and vast experience with all kinds of trouble, came up and sat down beside him and tried to talk about the horses, but Lou shook his head ruthlessly and went on making his plan. Then he got up slowly, smiled very coldly at Red Hertz, said, "I'll be seeing you," and was thinking, "I'll talk right to that priest's face and let him know where he stands. I've got my life, and he's got his. Everything used to go along smoothly enough."

Once again he looked around at his friends; not one could help him; not one of them had ever faced such a situation. So he left the poolroom, touching his hat as a polite gesture to two fellows who called out to him, and went out to the street, breathing much easier because there was a sound plan building itself up in his head. On the way back to the hotel he walked almost sedately, feeling like a very competent man.

The proprietor, who saw him coming in, beckoned to him. "Come here, Lou," he called. Mr. Baer, a man Lou admired, who had never been arrested for anything, had a very quiet manner, a cynical smile and talked usually in a whisper that sometimes got hoarse, but was always confidential. From the girls he firmly took money for the rooms, but still, if they had a bad week, he was not insistent, he gave them credit, and in this way kept them contented and yet always in debt to him. He never lost money, because he was such a good judge of a girl's character.

"What do you want, Mr. Baer?" he asked.

"You'd better not go upstairs. That priest is up there."

"That's fine," Lou said flatly. "Then I'm going up. He's the guy I want to see."

"What's the use of making trouble?"

"I'll not make trouble, only those girls may start taking him seriously. Then where do I come in? Where do you come in? I'm not the guy to take that lying down."

"I'm laughing, Lou. There's no chance of that."

"It would be fine if they didn't, but I don't like the look of him. You can't tell about priests. I don't like priests."

"Hey, Lou, come here. You're a sensible guy, a man like myself, that's why I like you. Listen to this. Don't make any trouble around here, and get this into your head. It's all the same to me whether they take a rabbit or a priest or a czar of Russia up there, so long as they make it pay. Do you see?"

Lou still felt strong and eager and capable of developing his own plan, but he glanced at Mr. Baer very cautiously and said, "Maybe you're right." So he did not go upstairs. He began to see that it was better to have Ronnie get as much money as she could from the priest, and while he smiled coldly at Mr. Baer, he began to weigh the profit from the transaction against the possibility of the priest persuading Ronnie to leave him. "I don't know what I'd do without the kid now. We're used to each other," he thought uneasily.

Then he grinned all over his face as he remembered suddenly, "Say, what would she do without me? What on earth would the kid do without me? She'd be weaker than a kitten." So then he felt absolutely sure of her and he smiled, showing his teeth, and stuck out his chest and began to swagger out to the street. He felt very strong and sure of himself again. He enjoyed this new strong feeling of security all the way back to the poolroom.

Thirteen

OFTEN FATHER Father Dowling stayed so late with the two girls it was embarrassing to have to go home, for the other priests had begun to notice that he sometimes came in after midnight. They were talking about him in such a way that the words they used barely trembled with the faintest, slyest inferences. Sometimes they even regarded him very thoughtfully. He was still giving money to Ronnie and Midge and sometimes little presents like chocolates and flowers, as though they were shy, timid girls. He had got to know when they were feeling gay or sorrowful and even when they were deceiving him, and knowing their weakness and shameless deceits so well only made him love them all the more. He could see that Midge was sick, for she had become thin and bad-tempered, but he dreaded to find out what was the matter with her, as though there were diseases that might mark the final depth of her degradation. His love for these two girls was so great now that he longed for them to remain always a part of his life.

When he was leaving them one night, they looked at him solemnly, glanced at each other, and Ronnie said, "I don't know what we'll do now, Father."

"What's the matter now, child? I thought you both seemed quite happy."

"Midge ain't feeling well, Father."

"I know. God help her. I was thinking about her last night. What's the matter with her?"

The girls looked at each other uneasily and finally Ronnie said, "It's a sickness you mightn't know about. It's like . . . I tell you what it's like, it's like a woman's trouble. That's it."

"Hasn't it a name? It must have a name."

"Then I don't know the name. It's just a complaint. Like a woman's complaint," Ronnie lied to him. "I'm sure you wouldn't know about it."

"She ought to see a doctor."

"She ought to go to a doctor and maybe go to a hospital and be looked after in proper style. If we only had a few dollars to last a few weeks it would make all the difference in the world. Don't you see what I'm driving at?"

Midge remained silent, staring at the priest mournfully, pleading with her round eyes like a child that hopes nothing will be denied her. Father Dowling was suddenly full of longing to be able to take the girls far away from the city, to free them once and forever, but he was helpless. His hand went mechanically to his pocket, he sighed and muttered, "I wish I could do something. I've nothing now."

"There's not much for us to do then," Ronnie said sullenly.

"What do you mean?"

"You can take three guesses about what it will have to be."

"We've got to do something," Midge said, hurting him ruthlessly even while feeling a bit of sympathy for him. She looked haggard, desperate, but she smiled slyly at Ronnie.

"It's a terrible situation," he said, rubbing the tips of his fingers on his cheekbone. He was trying to think of some place where he might get money. His foot began to drum nervously on the floor and then began a tapping beyond all control. His shoe was slapping on the carpet. "The main thing is, don't feel impatient. Don't feel uneasy. I'll help you. To-night or to-morrow night. Something will turn up," he said. He smiled so warmly and with such hope that they kept on grinning even after he had gone.

The priest's allowance was no more than fifty dollars a

month and from that sum he always put aside a few dollars to send to his mother. In the town where he had lived before going to the seminary, his family had been very poor, but his mother, a determined, ambitious woman, had longed for him to be a priest, and his brother, too, had wanted a priest in the family. So his brother had supported him and his mother during the long years at school. "I ought never to neglect sending money home. But I wonder what's the matter with Midge? She ought to be sent to a doctor." He kept on hearing Ronnie say, "There's nothing else for us to do. We've got to try and keep ourselves in some way." With sudden eagerness he tried to pretend to himself that his mother would approve of him giving money to the girls, although he secretly knew well that she would despise them without ever trying to understand them. In the last few months money that ought to have gone home to his mother had gone to the girls, and as he began to realize how he had neglected his obligation, he found himself thinking of those days when he had been a student and had gone home for the holidays. His mother waited on him with devotion; his brother brought him presents; the neighbors whispered that his family had no right to be spending so much money on an education for Stephen when they were so poor. It was all pride and vanity on the part of the mother, they said. Sometimes he himself had wondered whether his mother was a very pious or a very proud woman. But those evenings in the summer were fine and joyful, when he and his mother and brother sat on the front porch that was covered by the leaves from the big elm tree, and rocked back and forth lazily on their chairs while the boards squeaked and he answered their eager questions and they listened to the sound of the lake water lapping on the shore just beyond the end of the street. At such times he had felt their tremendous happiness, especially during those moments when they were silent. It had always been understood among them that when Stephen became a priest, he would support the mother and give his brother a chance to save some money.

As Father Dowling walked along, he began to remember what the town and the surrounding country would be like at this time of year, when the snow was going and there would be strong spring sunlight. All those northern hills beyond the town that were so blue in the summer time would now be bare and the sun would shine on the naked slopes and make them seem from the bay like fields of yellow wheat, and on top of the great hills the snow patches would remain to glisten brilliantly in the late afternoon. The bay and the lake would be intensely blue, but there would be the long white margin of broken ice along the shore.

It seemed terrible to Father Dowling that he had been neglecting to send money to his mother, who was so deserving of his love, and it seemed just as terrible that he had no money, either, for those whom he most wanted to help.

That evening he was hearing confessions. People who came to him at this time every week felt a strange aloofness in his manner. It was true that he listened as patiently as ever and sometimes even sighed sorrowfully, but his sighs hardly seemed to be for the sins of his penitents. And it did not occur to him to-night to scold them or work himself into an ardent passion in the way some of the women loved. Up until the time one young man came into the confessional he had actually let many penitents go away feeling that their sins were trifling and unimportant, and even this young man, for the first part of his confession, did not arouse the priest. He was a university student who was worrying about losing his faith: it seemed that he could not pray when he went into church, for his soul seemed to dry up and he felt uncomfortable and bored and sat in the pew arguing with the priest in the pulpit, and in his imagination making the priest appear stupid. There were times, too, when he felt that the Church, the visible church and the mystical body, was rotten at the core and always socially delinquent.

Father Dowling whispered, "Are you sure you're not

getting your notions from authors of books. Are you sure your reading doesn't tend to destroy your faith? What have you been reading?"

"I've been reading Marx and Engels and Nietzsche, Father."

"And you like Marx and Engels?"

"They have sometimes filled me with enthusiasm, Father."

Father Dowling hesitated, not knowing quite what to say, for he did not know these authors very well, but he began by saying, "What a great pity Marx was not a Christian. There's no reason why a Christian should not thirst after social justice. The Church is not tied up to any one economic system, in fact, all systems tend to degrade the Church by using it to pacify discontented people. They would make religion an opium for the people, and we must be ever on our guard to see that the laity and the clergy, too, are not becoming the tools of designing rulers and the class interests. There is nothing to prevent a priest speaking stupidly on matters that he does not understand. It is only in the confessional and on the altar that he must be heeded and his instructions followed. But for heaven's sake, have a little Christian charity; if you are at mass and you hear a priest in the pulpit talking nonsense, or what you feel sure is nonsense, don't sit there sneering at him. You don't have to listen to him. Get up and walk out. Smoke a cigarette outside and then go back when he's finished. Ah, my dear young Christian friend, it is indeed a disordered world. God help us all. There are so many remedies offered. Try Our Lord, why don't you? And there is no reason why you should be worried by Nietzsche, my son. I know he is not a Christian, but are you sure you are understanding him? Are you sure that there is not an emphatic spiritual declaration in Nietzsche? There is, my boy. He hates paleness. Man, for him, is not an end, he is a bridge. His was a martial spirit. Remember how he writes with passion and how he hates spiritual inertia. He hates paleness, too, I have said, and he would surely think that your mean shallow contemporary skeptics and atheists were dreadfully pale and woebegone. Perhaps even his lack of Catholicity is a disguise, and underneath this disguise there's much that a Christian can learn. Do you follow me?" Father Dowling, whispering rapidly, began to make the young man believe that he had not read the German writer correctly. When he had finished the priest thrust his face close against the wire grating and said, "Now do you understand?"

"Yes, Father."

"That's good. The grace of God will help you to see much further into the matter. Go on with your confession," Father Dowling said, leaning back.

"I committed fornication, Father."

"How many times?"

"Twice, Father."

"With a young girl that you seduced?"

"No, Father."

"Not with another man's wife, I hope?"

"No, Father. With a prostitute."

"Dear, dear, dear. Well, better with a street woman than with an innocent young girl or a married woman. You saw the same woman twice?"

"Yes, Father."

"You picked her up off the streets?"

"In the first place, Father. Then I liked her and went to see her again."

The next question came slow and hesitant from Father Dowling: he did not even know whether he should ask the question. "Was it in this neighborhood, my son? On the streets around here?"

"Yes, Father. It was."

As he sat up stiffly, Father Dowling felt absolutely sure that the young man had picked up either Midge or Ronnie; then he could not prevent his head from going forward and his eyes peering through the wire wicket into the dark corner where the boy was kneeling. But he could not see more than the back of the boy's head, so hidden he was, and as he breathed deeply, and heard the boy breathing steadily, too, it began to seem inevitable that those two girls should have been touching the life and soul of this young fellow and perhaps many others like him, touching in this piercing way the life of the whole parish. How close they all were together. Yet it was not until he had seen the girls apart from others and separately, that he had realized how united was all the life of his congregation, students, the mothers and fathers of students, prostitutes, priests, the rich and the poor who passed girls on the street and desired them. This exciting thought, which at first filled him with wonder, began to make him feel eager to be kind to the young man, who was whispering, "For these and all other sins which I cannot remember, I am heartily sorry, Father."

"For your penance say ten Our Fathers and ten Hail Marys, and now make a good Act of Contrition."

While the young fellow was muttering his prayer, Father Dowling was making the sign of the cross over him, and this motion with his hand in the air as he granted absolution became almost a caress, he was feeling such extraordinary tenderness for this penitent. Then he swung the panel across the grating and he was alone. He sat in the darkness, waiting for some one to come into the confessional, still hearing the scraping of the young man's feet, smelling the odors of stale face-powder, cheap perfumes, the mixed breath of many strangers, the smell of bodies confined in that small space, and as he listened, it all seemed good to him, like the teeming richness of living things.

And he began to realize more clearly than before, after having listened to the student, how important the souls of the two girls were to him. He realized that they required all his love, because he alone understood them, and saw that through them he could love the young man too, and every one else who touched them. "It certainly was better for that boy to have been with Ronnie or Midge than some pure young girl. It was probably Midge. Maybe there is some purpose in their life after all," he thought.

No one else came into the confessional, so he removed his

purple stole from around his neck and put it into his pocket, and he swung aside the curtain and walked out to the church aisle. He went out and stood on the Cathedral steps, feeling the cool night air and looking over toward the main streets where the sky was glowing bright with the electric sign reflections, where the traffic was rumbling, where the crowds were streaming out of the theatres and into the restaurants and dance halls. And in the small hotel room on the other side of the block, Ronnie and Midge were maybe waiting for him to bring them a little money.

He felt dreadfully tired. As he went into the rectory he passed Father Anglin's door, and he thought, "If something does not turn up by to-morrow, I'll speak to Father Anglin."

Upstairs, he talked for a few moments with Father Jolly about the ball teams in the spring training camps in the far south. In the summer time the two priests went to the ball games together, and tried to arrange it so they could motor to the city where the world series was being played. Father Jolly knew the pitching record of every pitcher who had been in the big leagues for at least two years. His small, eager, dark face, with big glasses, was full of animation as he talked. "Come on into my room and I'll give you a shot of rye and maybe we can get worked up to singing some songs," he said. "Not to-night. I feel restless," Father Dowling said, and Father Jolly, eyeing him shrewdly, knew that he was unhappy.

There was a sermon that still had to be prepared for the eleven o'clock mass to-morrow, and Father Dowling did not look forward to it with much enthusiasm. The pulpit had lost some of its attraction for him since he had been advised to avoid controversial social problems. But as he sat in his room with the night air coming in so freshly through the open window, he opened his Bible and found himself reading the Song of Solomon. And it began to seem to him as he leaned forward breathlessly that he understood some of the secret rich feeling of this love song, sung so marvellously that it transcended human love and became divine. Then he forgot how he had been worrying about borrowing money. He began to write rapidly. He smiled with exaltation. He prepared his sermon on human and divine love. The bold sensual phrases of the love song startled him, stirred him and were full of such meaning that he read them over and over again.

And in the morning he preached on the Song of Songs, only he made it a song of love that all people ought to have for one another. Words rolled out of him with passion, and his ardor was so great that many who listened felt uneasy. He had got thinner. His deep-set blue eyes were no longer mild, but full of defiance as he shouted out, "Many waters cannot quench love, neither can the floods drown it."

When mass was over he stood by the church entrance, bowing to men and women with a little more warmth in his smile than there had been for many weeks, for he was searching into their faces, wondering, "Which one of them will I speak to? Which one will be kind enough to give me something for Ronnie and Midge?"

Young men of the parish sauntered past him to the street, looked around to see who among their friends was at this mass and then went down to stand by the curb and light their cigarettes. Soon there was a long line of young men along the curb, all wearing their best clothes, all smoking and talking to each other. In the course of a year a priest gets to know the faces of many of his parishioners even when he forgets their names, he gets to know their voices, their thoughts, the little things that worry them. At the Cathedral there were, of course, a great many strangers from all over the city and from out of town, too, who just came once and never even noticed Father Dowling, but the old parishioners, like Mrs. Haley, the white-haired widow who wore the oddest bonnet with artificial pink flowers and who had such a rosy face, bowed very low to him. And Hahn, the doctor, with a morning coat on his hungry-looking body, squinted his sharp fanatical eyes and smiled coldly, too. And there were three young girls with arms linked, who glanced up charmingly, half flirting with

Father Dowling without knowing it. There was a little boy with an Eton collar, holding the hand of his sister, with long golden curls. They all kept coming out, hundreds of strange faces and a few he saw every Sunday; the rich ones at once began to look around for their cars; the jolly, poor women formed little groups on the pavement and began to chatter. A cripple, a Frenchman who had had rheumatism for twenty years, was being helped into his wheel chair. Father Dowling had never smiled more patiently, or looked at these people more shrewdly than this morning.

Then Mr. James Robison and his daughter passed by; the daughter, a slim, tall, dark girl who smiled good-naturedly at Father Dowling and nodded her head shyly. The lawyer, florid-faced and handsome in his morning coat and very amiable, with his face wreathed in smiles and a bit of morning sunlight touching his white hair, put out his hand heartily and said, "Good morning, Father. It was a great pleasure to listen to you this morning. Seldom have I heard such eloquence. Seldom have I been so moved."

"Then we don't disagree about the subject matter of the sermon this morning, Mr. Robison?"

"Oh, tut, tut, come now, Father. Who am I to disagree with you about such matters? All I can say is that love and charity always will seem to me to be the divine themes, the most powerful themes for affecting the human heart."

"I'm glad you were moved. I hope many others were, too."

"You may be sure they were. You gave us all something to think about," Mr. Robison said.

The handsome lawyer was more gracious, more humble this morning than he had ever been. Both he and his daughter seemed to be full of admiration for the young priest. A strange confidence, a sudden joyfulness surged through Father Dowling. Putting back his head, he laughed out so loud that everybody standing on the steps turned and smiled. It was always exhilarating to hear one of the young priests laughing in this way.

Father Dowling bent over and whispered to Mr. Robison. "I've a little matter I'd like to talk to you about. It would only take a few minutes this evening. I wonder . . ."

"Come around, Father. We'll all be glad to see you."

"If it's possible I'd like if we were alone."

"Fine, fine, fine," Mr. Robison said, shaking his white head in agreement.

For a few moments longer Father Dowling stood on the steps, smiling, looking down at the cement sidewalk, noticing no one, then he turned, the skirt of his soutane swung out like a sail, and he went hurrying up through the church.

Fourteen

THAT EVENING Father Dowling came down the path by the church, stood a moment on the sidewalk, as though making sure for the last time of an explanation, and started to walk rapidly up the street. When he passed under the light his red lips were still moving in time with his thoughts. It was a very fine night. At dinner-time he had hardly eaten anything; he had kept going over and over his plan.

The lawyer lived in an old, vine-covered stone house, one of the oldest houses in the neighborhood. As Father Dowling stood on the sidewalk looking up at all the lighted windows, he felt afraid, for he seemed to be risking so much. "If he will not come, or if he does come and won't help them, what will I do?" he wondered.

When James Robison came into the drawing-room, Father Dowling was walking up and down, his hands clasped behind his back, the excitement so strong in him that he smiled vaguely at the lawyer, trying to find great kindliness in his healthy face. He had decided to discuss the matter in an impersonal way, but as soon as he heard James Robison saying, "Gracious, Father, you look very uneasy. Won't you sit down and smoke a cigar?" he turned with his young face full of his intense eagerness and said, "Mr. Robison, you'll have to forgive my eagerness, but I want you to help some one. I want you to give some one a little money, just as much as you think is deserved. Are you in a position . . . do you think you might be willing?"

Far from being startled, Mr. Robison said, "Tut, tut," and beamed rosily, for as soon as the priest had spoken to him in the morning he had imagined that a contribution of some kind for some worthy charity was being solicited. On the way home from church he had even made up in his mind how much he might give; if it was a small, unobtrusive charity, he had thought he might suggest fifty, or a hundred dollars, a check he would write while chuckling to himself, glancing occasionally over his shoulder at the delighted face of the young priest. After that was done he had intended to offer Father Dowling a drink of very old, expensive wine and send him away full of good humor and praise.

So as he chuckled at Father Dowling now, he said, "Dear me, Father, what is it that I'm expected to give? Has Father Anglin something in mind? You know you don't give us folk much rest. But it's a blessing in a way to have you think of me. What is it, Father?"

"Do you remember those two girls I once spoke to you about?"

"You asked me to get jobs for them, I believe."

"Yes, they're the ones. They're the ones again to-night."

The smiling, ruddy-cheeked assurance which made Father Dowling's manner so agreeable, vanished as soon as he mentioned the girls; he was so desperately serious now that he was making James Robison uncomfortable, for the lawyer preferred the way the older priest asked for contributions, with a splendid aplomb, a fine, gracious exchange of compliments that set them both rolling with hearty laughter. "I've kept them in mind, Father. I've asked about jobs for them but there is little work these days," Mr. Robison said defensively.

"It's not a job I want for them now. I want some money for them. I want you to give it to them. I want you to come and see them and understand the situation and help them. Will you do it for me, Mr. Robison?"

The lawyer was irritated, for if he refused to see the girls Father Dowling could certainly accuse him of a complete lack of charity. But he resented being dragged from his house in this way. "Please come, won't you?" Father Dowling pleaded. "It will be a great personal favor to me, and certainly you'll please God. It won't take more than a half an hour, and I'll tell you all the special circumstances."

While still hesitating, Mr. Robison amused himself by fancying he could see himself and the priest walking into some poor girl's home like two benevolent patrons of the whole parish. There would be an old woman who would dust off a chair in great confusion. The man of the house would be ashamed of his unshaven face and become inarticulate. And while he was having these thoughts the priest was begging him to go with him. "I'll get the car," he said. "We'll drive there."

"No, let's walk. It's not more than fifteen minutes away," Father Dowling said.

"Why walk when we can go in the car?"

"It won't seem so grand, don't you see?"

"Ah, yes, quite true, quite true."

They went out together, with the priest leaning close to Mr. Robison, who walked erectly, carrying a cane, wearing a hard hat and a white scarf, and listening to the young priest with a judicial expression on his crisp, ruddy face. Father Dowling had wanted to appear grave and judicial, too, but as they walked along together he found himself taking hold of the lawyer's arm, talking impulsively about Ronnie and Midge, leaning forward so he could half see the lawyer's face, his words full of passion and conviction. Words poured out of him and he never stopped to wonder why the lawyer was not answering. He told about his first meeting with the girls, that night when he had gone to see them to help them, and all he had tried to do for them, and how he had worried and hoped to keep them off the streets. By this time they had left the good old residential district and were in the rooming-house neighborhood, and the lawyer was looking up anxiously at all the houses. The priest went on, "I've given all I can of my own money. I'd give more, but I'm no longer able to help them. I want you to do something for them. Somebody has to help them.

They must be kept off the streets. Don't you understand that?" he said. "I've worried so much about them. When you see them you'll like them as I like them. You may be just as anxious about them as I am."

"Where have you been seeing them, Father?"

"I've been going around to the hotel where they live."

"Is that where they do their entertaining?"

"You mean is that where they took men?"

"Yes."

"It is."

"Lord in heaven, Father. You haven't let people see you going around there, have you?"

"I've gone at night. Nobody has noticed me." Father Dowling got a bit excited and almost angry at the lawyer. "What would it matter if they had noticed me? Tell me that. Are there some places where a priest must not go, some people that must not be touched?" But he restrained his irritation and with extraordinary diplomacy said, "Of course, I understand your point of view. It worried me a good deal, too. You understand how it would worry me, don't you?"

"I imagine it would give you the gravest concern."

"It concerned me night and day."

"I'm glad you realized the implications."

Looking quickly into the young priest's face, Mr. Robison felt all his sincerity, he felt even some of his love, so he, himself, became uneasy and then gradually inarticulate. A moment ago he had been bursting with shrewd criticism, but now he kept thinking of the surprising eagerness and love he had just seen in Father Dowling's face. In spite of himself, he was curious to understand this love, this eagerness which did not seem like any emotion he had ever felt.

By this time they were near the old hotel with the broken sign. They were across the road, opposite the quick lunch, the counter lined with customers. Suddenly Father Dowling said, "This is the place. You come in with me. We'll go up and I'll introduce the girls to you and say you're thinking of helping them, eh?"

"Wait a minute, wait a minute, Father."

"What's the matter?"

"We shouldn't barge into this thing in such a rush," he said testily.

Mr. Robison looked up at the hotel with the darkened windows, the narrow entrance and the faded yellow bricks. The stream of light from the lunch-counter window, gleaming on a narrow strip of pavement, made the house next door darker and dirtier. He was uneasy and very cautious. "What a miserable little place," he said. "This is where you've been coming, Father?"

"It looks brighter on other nights when the barber shop is lit up."

"Maybe this isn't the right night for a visit, then."

"Nobody will notice you, Mr. Robison. Just follow me inside and up the stairs."

"No, no, Father. Leave go of my arm. I'll wait here. You go in. You know the place. If you find them tell them to come out. I don't really know that I ought to be here at all," he added irritably.

Father Dowling went into the hotel and up the stairs and he rapped on the white door. There was no answer. He was so impatient and excited that he began to pound on the door, listening, pounding, waiting, hearing only the beating of his own heart. He looked along the narrow, dimly lit corridor. "Why should they be out on such a night? Lord, don't let them be far away." He turned, sighed and came down the stairs very slowly, glancing toward the desk where the proprietor was sitting with the old imperturbable expression on his face, as if he hadn't even noticed the priest coming in. Father Dowling was so disappointed he forgot his contempt for Mr. Baer and he said ingratiatingly, "Excuse me. Could you tell me if the two girls went out?"

"Certainly, neighbor. They went out about fifteen minutes ago. Maybe one of them or both will be back at any time. Stick around. There's the Sunday newspapers over there."

"Thanks very much," Father Dowling said. "It's very

important that I see them. I'll loaf outside." And he went out and crossed the street to Mr. Robison, who was pacing up and down and muttering to himself. "They're not in," he said. "Not at this moment, anyway."

"Ah, well, maybe it's better that way." The lawyer was much relieved. "Some other time, Father. We tried, that's the main thing," he said. "Let's walk home together."

But the priest took hold of Mr. Robison's arm and said firmly, "We can't do that. They'll be back. They may be just a little piece away. Just let's walk up and down here for a few minutes, anyway." And he kept hold of Mr. Robison's arm as they went up the street. To make it appear like a normal everyday bit of parish work, Father Dowling began to make an impersonal conversation about other interesting matters, for instance, the possibility of a war in Europe and whether it might mean the collapse of European civilization; but having started such a conversation he listened without any interest to Mr. Robison's opinions, and his eyes kept shifting across the street, seeking out and trying to recognize the form of any woman far up the avenue, longing to see the girls, but dreading to find them actually on the streets. Silent, and in step, they walked on. Suddenly a cat darted across the road, slowing down, its tail sticking up stiffly, and from the other side of the road the cat watched them walking on.

And when they turned the corner by the hospital, Father Dowling saw Ronnie coming toward them, loafing, hunting. The sight of her in her old coat, with her head moving so alertly, filled him with such compassion that he stood still and held the lawyer's arm tight. "There's the tall girl I told you about," he said. "The poor kid. Look at her. Wait here a moment," and he hurried up to Ronnie and stopped her.

"Ronnie, I've been looking for you. It's important. Where's Midge?"

"Hello, Father," she said. She did not seem glad to see him. It was a good evening and she had expected, if she hustled, to do very well in such weather. "I have a date with a girl to-night, Father," she said.

"No, no, Ronnie. You must do as I say to-night," he said, taking hold of her arm. "The gentleman back there is going to help you. See him waiting there. I've told him all about you and Midge. Come and meet him now. Please be nice to him. Be a good girl, Ronnie," and the priest was pulling her along toward Mr. Robison, who was standing there with his head thrust forward aggressively. Ronnie stood two paces behind the priest, eyeing the prosperous lawyer, and when she was introduced, she stepped forward apprehensively. After one quick, shrewd glance, the lawyer dropped his eyes and said, "How do you do, Miss."

"Hello," Ronnie said.

"Father Dowling wanted me to meet you and your friend."

"You may meet Midge and you may not. You can't be sure about Midge."

They walked on again, the three of them now, going toward the lighted avenue, the lawyer walking near the curb, and next to him Father Dowling, and then Ronnie, who kept her head down and would not speak, and even dragged her feet. Father Dowling tried to make a conversation, but Ronnie was resenting the way Mr. Robison had looked at her. They kept on walking for twenty minutes, going right over to the avenue. From time to time Mr. Robison took out his watch and made an impatient clucking noise with his teeth. He was dreading the notion of the three of them walking down the crowded avenue together.

Then a man with a white beard, in an old tattered brown coat, stooped at the waist, and with his shoulders thrust forward, passed by and he was whistling loudly between his teeth and looking straight ahead.

"I've seen that poor fellow many times around here. Haven't you?" Father Dowling said suddenly to Mr. Robison.

"I've never seen him in my life before," Mr. Robison said shortly.

"Father's right. I've seen him five hundred times," Ronnie said bluntly. "That's Whistling Joe. He whistles when he sees a girl. He's a bit daffy."

"Very interesting," Mr. Robison said.

Father Dowling was hoping that they might meet Midge before the lawyer got into a very bad temper. He wished he could start an interesting conversation.

They saw Midge standing on a corner by a hosiery store that had a large plate-glass window. She saw them at once and came up looking quite pretty, smiling very slyly and winsomely at the well-dressed and prosperous-looking lawyer. Her face was no longer round. Her cheek bones protruded slightly, but her eyes were much bigger and rather brilliant. When she was introduced to the lawyer she made a little bow and said, "I'm awfully pleased to meet your friend, Father," and he couldn't help smiling at her. Her presence, her composure, made them all feel better. Father Dowling, starting to laugh, said amiably, "Now I just want us to have a conversation. I want Mr. Robison to take an interest in you girls. Perhaps we'd better go back to the hotel and sit down."

"No. Under no circumstances," Mr. Robison said hastily.

"What's the matter with the hotel?" Ronnie said. "Gee, you don't seem to be in a good humor to-night."

"I won't go into that place. That's settled."

"That's settled," Midge said. "What's the matter with you, Ronnie? Let the gentleman take us wherever he thinks best."

"Mr. Robison, I wonder if we could go up to your place," the priest said. "Perhaps you would prefer to go where you would have privacy and feel more at home." The lawyer shook his head sharply, but Father Dowling was tugging at his arm, pulling him a few paces away, while the girls watched very haughtily, and he was whispering, "Mr. Robison, I'd give a good deal if these two poor girls could go to your home. I'd give a good deal if they could see your daughter and see how lovely and fresh she is. In this simple way we might do more than all my preaching could ever do. Would you do that, Mr. Robison?"

"Good God, Father, have you lost your wits?"

"It's the kind of thing you can handle perfectly, Mr. Robison."

The lawyer was secretly pleased by the priest's compliment. They both turned and looked at the two girls, who were standing close together, shabby, awkward, full of doubt and suspicion. The stiffness went out of Mr. Robison's manner. Some of the warm good humor that was usually in him returned and he smiled broadly. Besides, he felt that he would be more secure in his own home, although he hoped that his wife would not come into the drawing-room.

"I'll get a taxi, Father," he said. "I'll just leave the whole thing in your hands and if you want to go to my home, we'll be glad to have you."

While he was out on the curb waving his hand for a taxi, Ronnie said to the priest, "Why should we go? He won't do anything for us. I could tell that as soon as he looked at me. He looked at me and made me hate him. He's an old bastard."

"Please, child, don't talk like that. Do it for my sake," Father Dowling whispered.

They got into the cab with Father Dowling sitting in the back seat between the two girls and Mr. Robison on the stool in front of them, his hands clasping his cane that stuck up stiffly. There were few words spoken during the short drive. Midge lit a cigarette, and in the match-flare light, Ronnie blinked her eyes, Mr. Robison opened his mouth but said nothing, and the priest jerked his head back and said suddenly, "Easter is a full week earlier this year. Does anybody know how you tell when it's Easter each year?" But when no one answered him, he sat back contentedly, full of fine expectations. For the first time he was taking the girls among his own people. For the first time they would go into a good home and feel the warmth and kindliness of his people, and he was secretly hoping that Mrs. Robison would be there because she was such a splendid woman.

There was not even any conversation when they reached the house and Mr. Robison led the way into the drawing-room. Father Dowling began to beam good-humoredly because he felt at home here, where he had so often played cards and where many important world problems had been discussed. After taking off his coat and hat, Mr. Robison listened a moment apprehensively and said, "Now don't be shy, girls, sit down for a moment and let's talk a bit. Father Dowling has been talking to me about you. I'm your friend, you know."

Midge and Ronnie were leaning close together on a small settee, their eyes furtively seeking out the splendors of the room. Sometimes they glanced appealingly at Father Dowling. Ronnie was still sullen and suspicious; Midge was peering at the furniture and rugs with the wonder and pleasure of a child. And sitting there with their faces heavily powdered and too brightly rouged and their lips so vivid, they did not look very respectable.

"Some dump," Midge whispered.

"What are we doing here?" Ronnie answered.

"I told Mr. Robison that things were not going very well with you," Father Dowling began quietly. He saw that the girls were uneasy. He pitied them and wanted to shield them from shame or hesitancy. He stood up. Walking over to them, he said, "Take off your coats, girls. Don't feel uneasy," and he helped them take off their coats and smiled encouragingly as they sat there in the good dresses he had given them. And his manner was so simple and confident that both girls smiled timidly, forgetting they had ever mocked him, feeling that he was some one who had been close to them for a long time.

"Now, just what is it you'd like me to do for the girls?" Mr. Robison said. He had lit a cigar and was regarding Father Dowling and the two girls very shrewdly.

"What they actually need is work. Or if an effort were

being made to get work for them, then they would need a little to keep them during that time. That's all. They're both very anxious to work. Aren't you?"

"Yes, Father," Midge said. "We're good, willing workers."

"Would you do domestic work?" Mr. Robison asked.

Both girls nodded and smiled. "Domestic work would just suit us," Midge said. She was feeling more confident. Then Father Dowling said quietly, "If you could give them something to keep them in a cheap room till work was found for them it would be a perfect act of charity. I know it's been a hard winter and I know it's been difficult for men like you, but think of the predicament of these poor girls. You've never turned us down whenever we asked for anything, Mr. Robison. I know you won't now. The depth of the requirement is great here. Ah, I know that a deep charity is required, too."

While the priest was talking in this way, Mrs. Robison had come into the room and was listening, with her slender white hands folded at her waist and her eyes shifting around the room in astonishment. She was a tall woman with a few beautiful white streaks in her hair, who was still slender, whose skin was soft and pink, and who wore a plain black gown with a very low neck. No woman in the neighborhood, or for that matter in the whole city, had a more charming manner or more self-assurance, and it had always been a great satisfaction to the priests at the Cathedral to see her so devout in observing all the feast days and holy days and giving splendid leadership to all her co-religionists in the nicest social matters: and she was without ostentation, too, for she went to the very early masses by herself, whereas her husband and daughter went to the solemn high mass at eleven o'clock and bowed and nodded to everybody. And as she entered the room and looked at the two girls and the priest, she pursed her lips and was a bit amused and might merely have said, "Good evening," and have left them, if her husband had not stiffened and remained rigid in his chair, with his face revealing many flustered expressions. "Hello, a conference?" she asked mildly.

"Two young friends of Father Dowling," her husband said, getting up to introduce the girls. The priest had jumped to his feet at once, beaming his admiration of Mrs. Robison with such heartiness that she couldn't help showing how pleased she was by wrinkling the soft, smooth skin around her eyes, putting out her very white hand and tapping his arm affectionately. "I'd like you to meet these two girls," he was saying. "It's very kind of your husband to take an interest in them. Miss Bourassa, and Miss Ronnie Olsen, two girls who live in our parish."

"In our parish? Really? This is a pleasure," Mrs. Robison said. There was a withdrawal and an aloofness in the way she bowed and appraised the girls so shrewdly. "Really? Are you friends of Father Dowling?" she asked.

Smiling broadly and with her head tilted to one side, Midge stepped forward, and in her most affected manner, because she hated the woman as soon as she found herself being appraised, she said, "It's a treat to set eyes on you, Madam. I'm sure we'll get on swell together, don't you think so?"

But Ronnie, standing up slowly, said with a kind of sober defiance, "Sure. We're friends of Father Dowling. We're good friends, lady. That's what I mean." And she swayed her head restlessly from side to side as though she found herself chained to the sofa and forced to wait.

"You probably have many interesting things to talk about, and you'll have to excuse me," Mrs. Robison said without trying to conceal her polite annoyance, and she went out after making sure that her husband understood by her bitter glance that he was to follow her.

"Just like that," Midge said. "That's a signal to get on your horse, Ronnie."

"She walks right in and puts the finger on us, Midge."

"If she puts the finger on me like that again I'll bite her," Midge whispered.

"What are you saying, girls?"

"Nothing, nothing, Father."

Then there seemed to be difficulty in making conversation. Father Dowling was feeling ashamed. Of course he had not liked the way the girls had spoken to Mrs. Robison, but he was even more ashamed of her contemptuous appraisal of them. In that one shrewd appraising glance of a luxurious woman accustomed to security, she had condemned the girls forever.

Mr. Robison, who was growing more ill at ease, said, "Excuse me just a moment. I'll be with you in a moment," and he left the room to see his wife.

As soon as he had gone, Midge said sharply to Father Dowling, "We're leaving here at once. Who does the old bitch think she is?"

"We shouldn't have come here," Ronnie said. "I hate the likes of people like her."

"I'll give her an eyeful," Midge said, "if she puts her nose in here again."

"Midge. Ronnie. Listen to me. Don't be rude to her. Wait just a little while," Father Dowling said.

"We're not blaming you, Father."

So they waited in silence and soon Mr. Robison returned, with his face flushed more brightly than ever, yet with a beaten look about him. There was something he evidently intended to blurt out as soon as he entered the room, but when he saw Father Dowling's hopeful face, he faltered and sucked his lips. "I wonder if we could discuss this matter some other time," he said mildly. "Some important affairs have cropped up. Or, listen here, let's assume the matter is all settled in a kind of way, and a little later on I'll have a talk with Father Dowling here." And then he muttered so only the priest could hear him, "My wife's a bit of a Bourbon, don't you see?"

"It's upsetting, upsetting to us all. Don't you worry, Mr. Robison. You'll do all you can, won't you?"

"All in my power. They're nice kids. The little one's kind of pretty, don't you think?"

But then from the door, Mrs. Robison called, "I've called a taxi for the girls, if you don't mind."

"That was very kind of you, Mrs. Robison," Father Dowling said. He had intended to be charming, but there was so much animosity in her wise gray eyes and such a contempt, too, for him, that he turned away angrily and wanted only to get the girls out of the house.

"Ah, yes. We really must leave now," Midge was saying. "It's been a great pleasure to be here for the evening, Mrs. Robison. You must come and see me some time. Do you mind me telling you how I love that beautiful white streak in your hair? I've heard people say that anybody with a white streak in the hair has somebody crazy in the family, but I never believed that." And laughing brightly she went over to Mr. Robison, taking short mincing steps, her left hand extended with the elbow crooked up and her fingers held high, almost level with her chin. "I know you'll be coming to see me some time. It was a treat to meet the wife after the way you've mentioned her so often to me . . ."

"Midge," the priest said sharply.

"Come on, Midge," Ronnie said. "It's time we left." Her heavy jaw was moving a bit as if she might cry, but she strode across the room, very angular, very sober and sullen.

With his mouth drooping open, Father Dowling stood at the front door and watched the girls walking to the taxi that was waiting on the road. He wanted to run after them and comfort them. They never once looked back. Then his desolation strengthened into a feeling of rage and he turned and stared at Mrs. Robison, who was standing beside him, waiting for him to speak, and when he did nothing but stare at her rudely with his face full of indignation, she said crisply, "I must say, Father, I don't thank you for bringing streetwalkers into my house."

"And I can hardly compliment you, Madam, on the charitable way you received them."

"Then we disagree."

"Just about as emphatically as I can make it."

"I might as well tell you I think the whole business too scandalous to be believed."

"And I've been more scandalized in this house to-night than I've ever been in my life."

"You probably haven't much experience in these matters. That's the trouble, Father," she said, smiling sarcastically. "It might, indeed, be a difficult thing for us to discuss. We're both feeling short-tempered. You meant well enough, I know, but if you would realize that all prostitutes are feeble-minded . . ."

"That's a sociological point of view. It's not a Christian point of view. I'm ashamed to have heard it from you."

"There's not much use discussing the matter. Some other time, maybe," she said.

"Now, if you want my opinion," Mr. Robison said with a fine gesture of affability, "we're taking the whole matter too seriously. Come on, Father," he said, tapping the priest's arm, and as he drew him out to the front steps, he whispered, "She's a bit of a Bourbon, I tell you, when she's aroused," and there was a little pride in his whisper, for he would never have been able to dismiss a priest in the way his wife had done. "Treat the whole thing as a bit of a joke and let's try and forget it," he said.

Father Dowling felt that they had given him his hat and put him out of the house, just as though he were the neighborhood nuisance. Even when he reached the sidewalk, he kept glaring back at the house, and as he walked, his anger and disgust alternated so sharply that he did not realize he was back at the Cathedral till he looked up and saw the spire and saw, too, the cross at the peak thrust up against the stars and felt no sudden affection but just a cool disgust, as if the church no longer belonged to him.

He hurried to his room and began to undress rapidly, but gradually his motions became slower till at last he sat heavily on the bed. He pulled off his shoes, and then stopped, still bending down, listening, trying to remember; there was some one moment, a few words said during the evening he groped now to hear again; he heard Midge's voice and Ronnie's voice and Mr. Robison's, too, and almost every sound he had heard on the streets and coming from the boys on the corner. A snatch of conversation came up from the street below. . . . "He said take a ten per cent cut and I said I've already taken three cuts and I've got a wife and kids, and he said take it or quit, what are you going to do, and I said I got some independence and I'll quit, but first I'm going to punch you right on the nose, so I popped him one." As he still groped for that one moment, Father Dowling began to think that the whole city for years had been whispering its story to him out of the darkness in snatches, in a huge confessional where he could not see the faces: "Yes, I want to be a Catholic but I don't want to have any more kids and the priest says you can't practise birth control and be a Catholic, so you'll have to leave the Church. I said to him, if you had all the kids I had you wouldn't be so hardboiled, I'll bet you ten cents, and anyway I'm a sick woman and what can I do?" Her voice faded away and became simply a part of the hum, faded into the strong, confident nasal voice, "Sure he was my old man and I stole from him, but he had plenty and look how often I saw him slug my ma when she asked for anything, so I grabbed all I could and lit out when he tried to stop me, and I don't feel sorry that he died. Maybe I do feel sorry. Yes, I guess I do a little or I wouldn't be here." While Father Dowling was imagining he was remembering these voices coming from underneath the stirring and hum of the life outside, he was really still groping for that one voice, those few words; then he heard them clearly in Mrs. Robison's crisp tones: "Feeble-minded girls. Only feeble-minded girls go on the streets." Then his thoughts came flowing steadily. "The social service point of view, the unfit produce the feeble-minded, let's sterilize the feeble-minded, Mary Magdalen was feeble-minded and Mary of Egypt, too, and Joan of Arc heard voices; it becomes simply a problem of breeding, once you can sterilize the unfit it's easy to breed the whores out of existence, and the mentally fit are always moral, and immorality is simple feeble-mindedness. Mrs. Robison, Father Anglin, prominent women of the parish . . ." The darkness within him and the deadness became so deep he could hardly move.

Dragging himself over to the window, he looked out over the city. "I don't blame Ronnie and Midge, whatever they're doing," he thought, for he felt sure that at this hour they would be walking the streets. He looked out over the roofs and lights and noises on the streets, over the corners where on Sunday evenings evangelists sang, and over that street where the crowd at this moment was streaming from the labor temple; somewhere out there where the lighted avenues lengthened and the streets criss-crossed, the girls were loafing and hunting. He felt full of love for them and sometimes he looked up at the stars.

Fifteen

ALL THAT evening Mrs. Robison, in her most caustic manner, urged her husband to call on the Bishop and warn him that the young priest was apt to precipitate a scandal that would shame every decent Catholic in the city. Never had she discussed a matter with such passionate conviction. Father Dowling had implied by his indignation a contemptuous criticism of her manner of living and her spiritual and social life, and the more she pondered, the more she felt with deep sincerity that he was misguided, and the more she was determined to cling desperately to her faith in her own wisdom.

Her husband listened to her arguments, reasoned with her, sometimes like a naïve boy, and made many illogical objections, whereas all the time he knew he was not worrying about his wife's wounded vanity. "Now you mark my words, James. You're supposed to be a man of fine judgment in business. I'm simply saying, use your good judgment here in this case," she said. It was the first time in years that her security and poise had ever been challenged, and in one way, her husband, listening to her, wanted to duck his head and chuckle, but it was his own conscience and his own sense of duty that was disturbing him. If there was one thing more than another that he objected to, it was scandal that might affect his position in the community, and as a prominent citizen he had always felt it was his duty to cherish the good name of his religion, especially in this very Protestant community. But supposing Father Dowling was arrested with these two women? Supposing he was hauled into a police court . . . a fallen priest, immersed in the lives of two prostitutes? What was his duty? Of course a good Catholic ought always to shelter and protect his priests . . . no one on earth was so close to God. Once at an ordination sermon, he had heard an exuberant old priest shout out that the young priest was just as pleasing to God as the Blessed Virgin. Complaining to the Bishop might be a little like striking at a priest. "It would be something like hitting a priest," he said to his wife.

"Supposing a priest were mad. Wouldn't you restrain him and use force to do it?" she asked.

"Don't be silly," he said. "I've got nothing against him." But he was remembering that once at college when he was being initiated and was being beaten by the boys, he had swung his fist and they had yelled, "He hit a priest. Oh, my God. Kill him," and they had started to beat him harder than ever, and blindfolded as he was, he had wept until he heard their mocking laughter. "Now," he reasoned irritably, "it's not up to me. It's up to the Bishop. Something has to be done."

The next morning at the breakfast table, Mrs. Robison was graver and more meditative than usual, and she would have liked to continue the discussion, only the presence of their daughter, Celia, chattering briskly and laughing, made such an ugly conversation rather difficult. All Mrs. Robison could do was throw one worried glance after another at her husband, whose rosy face was grave and full of resolution.

Mr. Robison was still thinking as he had thought all last night, "Who is Father Dowling? Where does he come from? What do I know about him?" He was trying to get rid of a peculiar regretful sympathy he felt for the young priest whom he had always found amusing in a harmless way, or maybe it was that he was still trying to get rid of that last bit of the disturbing feeling he had had going along the street with the young priest last night, when words had poured from him as he told of a love that was puzzling and hard to understand. "Maybe I oughtn't to speak to the Bishop till I understand the nature of his feeling," he thought, and then he remembered, "But he always had too much to say. He seemed to be looking for trouble. He's always been tainted with dangerous thinking. His sermons against what he calls the bourgeois world. Always putting his head into situations he doesn't understand. A creature of excess. He'll make fools of us all. Lord knows what he's doing with those women and trying to get me to keep them for him."

That morning, from his office, he phoned the Bishop. In the afternoon he drove up to the Bishop's palace. The palace was an old, dirty, gray-stone building, not far away from the Cathedral. Even when Mr. Robison was standing on the steps in the sunlight, ringing the door-bell, he hesitated and fussed with his coat lapels. He looked very dignified in his hard hat, showing the white hair against his rosy cheeks, and in his dark coat with the velvet collar, and his cream-colored gloves in the hand that held his cane. Just as the door was opened for him, he suddenly felt that he liked the young priest and would not willingly hurt him. It was actually like a mild feeling of humility, that feeling he had standing on the steps in the sunlight, but then he remembered that he was doing a painful duty and he felt a bit more cheerful.

He was shown into the library, where Bishop Foley was smoking and waiting. The Bishop was nearly seven feet tall, with great broad shoulders and thick dark hair. He was a man who was respected by everybody in town who knew him. He had a big, round, heavy, dark, threatening face, and he was inclined to be a bit of a bully, although when it was necessary, as it was now when he put out his hand to Mr. Robison, he had a very charming manner. And he had a fine mind for politics, an intuition that compelled him to do the expedient thing, and this gift had advanced him rapidly in the Church, where he was supposed to be an administrator rather than a contemplative. Coming from poor people, he never could get used to the notion of luxury, and he used to walk long distances in the cold winter to save a few cents rather than take a cab. Every time he appeared in a pulpit and shouted in his great rolling voice, or sang the midnight mass in his splendid robes, with his towering height at the altar, people like Mr. Robison were much impressed; and the same people were likewise proud of him when he was on a platform with ministers of all denominations in a public cause which required him to look concerned, which he could do easily because he hardly ever smiled.

He shook hands enthusiastically with Mr. Robison, for they had had many fine conversations together, particularly when they were planning a financial campaign. Sitting uneasily on the edge of his chair, Mr. Robison took a deep breath and said, "I'm sorry, Your Grace, but I'm afraid this conversation will be painful for both of us. It has been worrying me all afternoon. I'm speaking to you with great reluctance and only in view of our old friendship."

"Surely nothing can be as serious as that sounds," the Bishop said, chuckling.

Then Mr. Robison realized with both relief and mild disappointment that nothing he could say would in any way shock this bishop, or disturb the immobile aloofness of his heavy sombre face, or make his eyes do anything more than shift around shrewdly while he listened. A bit of sunlight coming from the window touched his heavy red lips, which were so softly caressing a cigar while he waited patiently, as if the lawyer needed a good deal of time.

"It wouldn't be so serious if it were about myself. Only I'm going to talk about some one else."

"I've never heard you speak harshly of anybody."

"I don't want to be harsh now, but there's a good deal involved."

"Who is it you have in mind?"

"A priest."

"A priest?"

"Yes, a young priest. And that's the difficulty."

"Before mentioning any names, Mr. Robison, do you mind telling me if the young priest is in trouble?"

"I think he's in very grave trouble, trouble that doesn't just touch him but may touch us all."

Both men nodded their heads understandingly. Then Mr. Robison, looking more worried, hesitated and found it hard to actually mention Father Dowling's name. "Your Grace," he said suddenly, "maybe it might be better just to tell you what happened, and then if you want to, you can ask for the priest's name." And leaning forward, talking slowly, he told how the young priest had taken him to the hotel and brought the two girls to the house and how the priest explained that he had been going night after night to see them, giving them money, giving them clothes and growing very fond of them. "And they were more than friendly with him," he said. "They were very much at home with him. I must say it gave me a very funny feeling watching them with him. Now I'm not saying he wasn't trying to help them . . ."

"What makes you think he wasn't helping them?"

"Well, you can use your own judgment, Your Grace. When we couldn't find them at the hotel, we went out looking for them on the street and there they were walking the streets."

"What did they actually want from you?"

"Money."

"Umph."

"I don't care about them wanting money. I'd give them money. But I don't want to contribute to a public scandal for the amusement of the whole city."

"Tell me the young priest's name, Mr. Robison."

"Father Dowling at the Cathedral. A likeable chap, too."

The Bishop nodded his big head and sighed deeply, as if the sound of the priest's name had made him very sad, but what he actually was thinking of as he looked out the window so gloomily, was not of the priest but of a charity campaign he was about to launch throughout the city, and he was imagining the result of a scandal that would follow if a priest were implicated with two prostitutes. Sitting there, he could almost hear the story spreading and growing throughout the city, appearing first of all half hidden in the newspapers, and then whispered about till it became a matter for obscene joking. This was not the first time that a young priest had worried him; only a month ago one of them had got drunk and had driven an automobile into a parked car, smashing it up, and he had been arrested, and it had been necessary to have the matter adjusted very quietly. So the Bishop, sighing again, said patiently to Mr. Robison, "I wonder if many people understand the temptations that continually confront a young priest. They're human beings, young men without much guile or experience, full-blooded and healthy, right out of the seminary into a world where many silly women dote on them. And yet the priesthood doesn't want them if they're not normal sexually, otherwise there would be no purpose in the vow of celibacy. It's astonishing to realize how few of them go wrong, isn't it? It would be impossible without the special grace of God. The greater the temptation, the more abundant the marvellous grace to strengthen them. Extraordinary, isn't it, Mr. Robison?"

"Indeed it is astonishing, Your Grace," Mr. Robison said. But his face began to redden and he looked a bit angry, as though he were being rebuked, or as though he were being teased, and he remembered having heard it said that the Bishop spent many secret hours studying the modern philosophers, so he would always know more than the brilliant young men who tossed quotations at him. But then the Bishop added, "Such a state of affairs as you outline can't be allowed to continue, of course. Heaven only knows what might happen."

"Ah, I'm glad you agree with me, Your Grace."

"I agree with you entirely, Mr. Robison. I might say I know of no one I would rather have bring me this information. And I've got a pretty good idea that it worried you a good deal."

"It upset me all last night, and I gave it plenty of consideration this morning, too. You know Father Dowling is a fine enough fellow in many ways. It's a shame, a ghastly shame."

"By the way, Mr. Robison, you have possibly some connection through the courts with the police?"

"You're suggesting, Your Grace . . ."

"Dear me, it's hard to say what to do. It's a pity the police wouldn't arrest the girls and get them out of the way. Maybe we ought to pray for that."

"We will, Your Grace."

"Ah, we should forgive these young priests for having a little too much enthusiasm. They ought to have it. Let me know if you hear anything about the girls. And I know you'll mention the affair to no one."

"I hesitated to mention it even to you."

"I know it. You're a good fellow," and standing up and smiling, the Bishop said, "How is Mrs. Robison? Be sure and remember me to her and tell her we must have a game of bridge some night." And while they were both standing up, he suddenly switched the conversation and began talking about the possibility of the Chinese offering stubborn resistance to the Japanese invasion. "I've heard missionaries say that the Chinese make the best soldiers in the world," he said. "That is, for trench warfare, because of their ineffable patience." And as he talked in this fashion, Father Dowling seemed to have been forgotten, as an insignificant detail in a great plan is quickly passed by, and even Mr. Robison, chatting affably, began to feel that he had worried himself needlessly. After one or two dry jokes about political matters, the two middle-aged men put out their plump white hands, bowed to each other and the Bishop said, "Be sure and say a little prayer for me."

Out in the sunlight, with his hat tilted cockily on one side of his head, Mr. Robison strutted along, holding his cane stiff in one hand, like a man who has come from an important and successful conference. But when he was at the corner, looking around for a cab, he suddenly remembered again the young priest's eagerness and his enthusiasm talking about the girls that night. And then he became uneasy, flustered, and irritable.

Instead of going back to his office, Mr. Robison went to his club for a cup of coffee, so he could relax and get rid of his uneasiness. And as soon as he stepped into the lounge room and saw a few of his white-headed cronies half buried in deep leather chairs, smoking, laughing, or dozing until they dropped forward, he knew that he had been wise in seeing the Bishop. If there were scandal these men, his business associates, would tease him slyly for weeks.

Sixteen

AFTER MASS in the morning, Father Dowling was ashamed of the way he had been thinking of the parish people the night before. He ate breakfast with Father Jolly and Father Anglin, looked a long time at the old priest's severe, weary face and made little conversation with either one of them. As they ate, he knew they were looking at him as though he were gloomy and haggard. Father Jolly, who was very fond of music, talked a lot about a concert he had attended. Father Anglin once asked Father Dowling if something were bothering him and waited for an answer with his blue eyes blinking steadily.

In the early afternoon he hurried to the hotel and rapped on the white door and waited, and when there was no answer, he went back to the street and stood in front of the hotel, with his hand up, shading his eyes from the sunlight, wondering where he might find the girls. As he walked slowly around the block, looking on the streets and through restaurant windows, he was thinking, "Wherever they are, whatever they're doing, God would forgive them now."

Before he went home, late that afternoon, he called on Mrs. Canzano, a poor Italian woman, bulging with her twelfth child. Her husband was out of work, and he tried patiently to instill into the poor woman a Christian resignation to a life of misery.

Early that evening he was ready to go again to the hotel, but he received a call to the bedside of old Mrs. Schwartz, that old lady whom he had visited that winter night when he first met Ronnie and Midge; only this time the old woman was really dying. He knelt beside her, praying for her, he stroked her head so lightly that her eyes were full of wonder. There were no shouts from her, no struggle as there had been on that other night, no fear, just a fixed simple smile on her face as he anointed her, and then she died very peacefully.

The way this old woman had died was still in his mind, making him calmer, when he went later that night to the hotel. When he was on the stair the proprietor looked at him in a certain way, a half smile, and Father Dowling knew that the girls were in the room, and he rapped on the door lightly with sureness and eagerness. But the door was opened only a few inches and he heard Ronnie say "Who is it?"

"I want to see you, Ronnie," he said.

A few inches more the door was opened, and Ronnie, smelling of cheap perfume and perspiration, and with her hair mussed over her head, said sullenly, "You'd better go away. You can't come in here any more."

"I'll wait, then," he said.

"You ought to go away and leave us alone," she said, closing the door.

Waiting, listening to every sound that came from the room, he walked up and down the narrow corridor, and sometimes he heard a laugh, and he said, "That's Ronnie," and sometimes he heard a man's voice and he frowned. As he kept on walking, his own footfalls sounded dreadfully loud, so loud he thought they made it hard for him to hear Midge's laughter. She was in one of those rooms. Then these sudden wild noises that he sometimes heard and sometimes imagined began to make him feel so unhappy that he tried to tread more heavily so his footfalls would drown out all other sounds. He thought of the peaceful death of old Mrs. Schwartz just a few hours ago. "Death and life, death and life. Where is the beginning and where the end?" he muttered. "What did I expect the girls to be doing? What else was there for them to do? God help them. Last night they were insulted and hurt. I can't blame them if they hate the whole city."

Then the door opened and he hurried along the corridor and almost bumped into the swarthy, short, fierce-faced man with shiny black hair and yellow teeth, who was coming out of the room. Mumbling something, the man turned, scared, and darted down the stairs, looking back once in spite of his fright.

By this time Father Dowling had his foot in the door, and he pushed his way into the room against the weight of some one pushing from the other side. There was Ronnie, breathing heavily, in an old green kimono and a pair of silk stockings and green pumps, and her hands were on her hips and her head was wagging from side to side in complete disgust. "For the love of Mike, Father," she said. "Why don't you leave us alone? You got your nerve pushing in here."

"Ronnie, Ronnie, just a minute. I only want to say how sorry I am for last night. It was my fault taking you there."

"Forget it. You don't think I'm sitting here worrying about your friends, do you?"

"He's not my friend, he never was."

"No? Never mind. He may get drunk and stumble in here some time, then he can go to church and tell you about it."

"Listen, Ronnie, I may have made a mistake and I embarrassed you and Midge. I had the best of intentions. Forgive me, won't you?" Coaxing, he smiled and put out his hand and touched her arm.

Frowning, as though he were a reckless young person and she did not know what to do with him, she sat down on the bed. Then she looked at the door leading into the other room and she wished he would go. As she lay back and crossed her legs, he could see a two-dollar bill showing through the silk stocking just below her knee. He could see the figure "two" quite clearly. His face, flushing at first, suddenly got white. Following his glance, Ronnie looked down at the two-dollar bill and grinned. "That's the gent that just went out," she said.

"I bumped into him," the priest said, dropping his glance to the floor.

"He didn't hurt you, did he?"

"Please don't talk about him, Ronnie."

Then there was the noise of laughter in the other room, Midge's laughter, and then other horrible sounds, and Father Dowling, thinking of Midge being sick and yet having some one in there, moistened his dry lips, went to speak, faltered as he stared at Ronnie, and listened and waited while she stared at him, his mouth opening and waiting for words to come from him, when there was only within him a shame that was making him die.

"I told you you'd better go away," Ronnie mumbled angrily. "What are you sitting there for if you don't like it?"

"I came to see you both and I'm waiting, that's all," he said. And then he smiled suddenly as if he were encouraging her, and he surprised her so that she shrugged her shoulders, said, "Suit yourself. Have your own picnic," and then looked at him with wonder.

Without any warning the other door was opened all of a sudden, and a huge, fat Italian, in a good navy-blue suit, his dark face beaming with an everlasting satisfaction, his dark eyes shining with new life, came out laughing and shaking his head happily. He must have weighed two hundred and fifty pounds. His name was Al Spagnola and he was in the fruit business. With one great expansive sigh of contentment that included Ronnie and Father Dowling, whom he hardly noticed, he walked across the room and out to the hall.

Father Dowling was astonished and angry because of the man's brazen, laughing contentment. "A big pagan, a happy animal. I seem to have seen him some place before. Just an earth worm, a barbarian right out of pagan Rome two thousand years ago," he thought.

Midge, leaning lazily against the doorpost, watched the

priest and puffed slowly at a cigarette. Her face was pale and calm. For a long time she stared at Father Dowling and then smiled just a little bit as though he amused her in some secret way she would never reveal. And then she snapped at him: "You haven't got the gall to come around here to-night nagging at us, have you?"

"I don't want to nag, Midge. What makes you think I want to nag? I'm apologizing, not nagging. I came around here so you could nag at me."

"I didn't think you'd put your nose around here again."

"I don't know why you'd think that."

"You had us insulted. You had us treated like dirt."

"That's why I want to apologize, don't you see, Midge? That's all I can do. If you don't want me to call on you again, all right, but you had an apology coming to you anyway," he said.

When the girls saw that the priest was not angry with them, nor disgusted at finding them with men, they grew ashamed and looked at each other foolishly. By this time both girls were sitting together on the bed. Father Dowling was smiling patiently. "All I say is you shouldn't have come in here when we were busy," Midge said, as though defending herself.

"You shouldn't let that worry you, Midge. Look here. I'm not worrying about it at all. I can forgive you for that to-night. You were provoked and bitter in spirit. Let's be friends again, eh?" he said.

But the girls could see that while he was forgiving them, the hurt remained very deep in him, for while he pleaded with such smiling eagerness, he was white-faced and halting sometimes in his speech. All last night and to-day, too, whenever they had mentioned him, they had jeered and joked at him, but now they couldn't sit there at ease and look at him when he was so full of humility. They both began to remember that they liked him very much; they wished he would not go on pleading with his eyes so silently, or keep making it so clear that he forgave them willingly.

"We're not blaming you for anything, Father. What made you think we were? What put that idea into your head?" Midge said.

"Oh, hell, we know there's nothing wrong with you, Father," Ronnie said.

"That's fine. Maybe you think everything I've ever recommended to you is pretty shallow, I mean you think the people I've respected are pretty shoddy."

"I'm not holding your lousy friends against you. You got used to them, I guess. We're not going to snoot you because of those mugs."

"You get used to anything," Ronnie said. "But you shouldn't play around with people like those Robisons. When you get down to brass tacks they're dirt. I wouldn't give that old hussy a tumble if I dropped from a parachute right on her knee. Don't get me wrong. We're whores and we know we're whores, but she's a different kind of a whore. See what I mean? Don't let her worry you, that's all."

"I knew you'd be bitter to-night. I don't blame you for your resentment," he said.

Looking puzzled, the girls shifted their bodies awkwardly on the bed and did not answer. He added simply, "That's why I wanted to be with you to-night. Do you mind if I stay a while?"

He was so friendly, he seemed to like them so much that they felt vaguely pleased and they did not want to offend him. As he talked mildly, he was locking the fingers of one big hand into the fingers of the other, smiling at them sometimes with that curious diffidence that always puzzled them.

"What do you want to do, Father?" Midge asked.

"Just stay here a while with you," he said, laughing.

"All right, that's easy. In that case I'll get dressed," Midge said. She started to go to the other room. Then she turned, because she liked him and knew how often he worried about her and because this kind of friendship seemed so very rare, and she said, "I'm sorry, Father, that you saw me like this." And she went into the room to get dressed.

Father Dowling began to smile warmly as he walked up and down the room, for his whole being was full of hope as he kept thinking, "How simple she was when she said that. What a fine simple regret. She'd be such a beautiful child under different circumstances. She'd have such understanding, too, and a far deeper understanding than so many superficially polite women have." As he paced back and forth, he smiled with relief, and Ronnie, who was watching him, full of curiosity, said, "What are you thinking about, Father? What do you find so funny?"

"I was thinking of Midge."

"Thinking what about her?"

"Just about the way she turned at the door."

"Do you love her?"

"In the same way I love you."

"But you don't smile like that when you think of me?"

"I often think of you. I always see the two of you together in my thoughts."

But she smiled at him very skeptically, as if she had a secret she would not tell, and when she was smiling, having this thought, she looked good-natured, easy-going and not at all stubborn or sullen, though her face was powdered thickly and her lips were a livid streak.

As soon as Midge returned to the room, Father Dowling asked them if they were hungry. "I've got a dollar in my pocket," he said. He wondered if they might get some sandwiches and coffee at the lunch counter on the street and have the food there in the room. "I'll go down and get the stuff for you," Midge said, and they all began to laugh as though they were looking forward to having a very good time.

While Father Dowling was opening the windows wide to let the fresh air into the room, Ronnie had taken a bottle of cheap red wine out of the bureau drawer. Midge came back with the sandwiches wrapped in a white napkin, and a big steaming coffee pot. The priest insisted on waiting on the girls; he poured the coffee for them, he put the sandwiches on the saucers, he wanted them to like the food. "This is the first time we ever ate together," he said, and he seemed very pleased.

And they used the coffee cups for the wine, too, and he poured the wine for them with a special graciousness, as if he were a host at a banquet. Then he began to talk about food, about savory dishes he had tasted, about recipes he knew by heart, about cheese and wines that had "a mysticism all their own," as he put it. The girls kept looking at each other and wanted him to go on talking. He remained very late. He would not go home while there was any chance of them going out on the street. All the time he was talking he was trying to think of some one who might loan him money without asking questions. The girls began to get sleepy. It was very late when the priest went downstairs. Even the proprietor had gone to bed.

Seventeen

ON THIS NIGHT it was damp and cold and the streets were deserted, so Midge returned to the hotel. Her clothes were wet and she was chilled to the bone. She opened the white door and walked into he room. She saw two detectives talking to Ronnie and laughing. Cringing behind Ronnie was a worried little man with a thin, hatchet face, who looked as if he was going to cry. As Midge walked in, this little fellow was saying, "This guy Lou tells me to rap on the door and just ask for Ronnie and that's God's truth."

When Ronnie saw Midge she put her hands up to her head and sat down slowly on the bed, and one of the detectives, the big, fair-faced, blue-eyed fellow in the hard hat, grabbed hold of Midge and said, "Here you are, baby. We're just holding a little surprise party waiting for you," and he started to shake her roughly and watch her head sway from side to side on her shoulders.

But Midge neither smiled nor wept. She just said, "What's the use of being so tough?" and sitting down beside Ronnie, she asked her, "What happened?"

"I don't know. These guys just walked in."

The two policemen began to joke at the two girls and jeer at the little fellow who had really begun to cry. "Doesn't he look like the answer to a woman's prayer, Joe? I'll bet he never has to pay a girl. They probably pay him," one said. Then they pushed him one way, and then pushed him back again. And they kept this up till Midge said wearily, "Oh, leave the guy alone, why don't you?" So the cops turned roughly on the girls. Ronnie jumped up and started kicking at them with her heels while Midge sat there full of hate, but too scared to move.

"Take it easy, Sam," the smaller detective in the light overcoat said. "We've got nothing much against these kids."

Scratching his head thoughtfully, the big, fair fellow said, "That's right. Maybe you're right at that, Joe. I never looked at it in that way," and turning to Ronnie, he said, "What's the use of making trouble, sister?"

"All right. Keep your hands off me, that's all," she said.

Every one in the room was silent and peaceful now while they waited, and then Midge, who was sitting rigid with her hands in her lap and her face white, suddenly began to cry. She did not know what was the matter with her, except that she felt weak and was trembling; and as she kept on wishing she could stop crying, she was steadily hating herself, for she knew that Ronnie was resenting such an exhibition of weakness. Pleading for something she herself did not understand, she said to Ronnie, "Please don't let me bother you, kiddo. What are we waiting for?"

Nodding laconically to the girls, the fair detective thumbed toward the door, and when they got up, he stood between them, holding their arms and whispering, "Mind now, kids, no fuss. Take it easy," and with the other detective following with the little man, who was still pleading desperately, they went downstairs to the desk. And there was the proprietor, red-faced, expostulating, shaking his fist and cursing to an enormous detective who was smiling good-naturedly and saying, "You'll have lots of time to talk about that to-morrow."

Then they all went out to the street where a small crowd had gathered on the sidewalk and on the road around the open door of the police wagon. A thin, misty rain, making the lamplights dim and the streets glisten, was falling on the upturned faces of the crowd. Lights from the barber shop shone on the open wagon door. Ducking their heads down in the collars of their coats, the two girls were pushed toward the wagon, but at the curb Midge slipped and fell, hurting her knee, and some one in the crowd started to laugh. The girls were helped into the wagon along with the proprietor and the sobbing little man.

On the drive over to the station no one spoke. The wagon began to smell of steaming wet clothes. Midge was beside Mr. Baer, who had his hands folded angrily across his chest, and next to him, only huddled by himself in the corner as if he dreaded the contamination that would come from sitting close to one of the girls, was the little lean man who had asked at the door for Ronnie.

At the station they were put in separate cells, but just before they were separated, Ronnie whispered to Midge, with her voice breaking with anxiety, "You don't think Lou's in wrong, too, do you, Midge? They couldn't do anything to Lou, could they?" On her angular face there was fear and desperate unhappiness. All the time in the wagon she had been thinking of Lou, for if Lou remained secure and free there somehow seemed to be so much to hope for.

And even when Midge was alone in the cell she was still thinking how foolish it was of Ronnie to worry about a man like Lou. "He'd bleed her to the bone. He'd pick the last scrap of flesh from her bones and then roll her over with his boot." And having these thoughts, and feeling terribly tired and without any hope, she sat there till a policeman came to the cell door, peered in, tramped back along the corridor and then returned with another cop who said, "She's not bad at all, heh? Heh, cutie, come here." They both laughed hoarsely but they couldn't get her to notice them. "Maybe you want a lawyer, little one," they said. "No, thanks," she said bluntly. She cupped her chin in her hands and put her elbows on her knees until they went away.

"Maybe it might help to get Father Dowling," she thought. "Maybe he could get us out. But no, he couldn't, and it wouldn't do any good and I couldn't stand the way he'd feel and have that hurt look on his face. There was that look on his face the other night. I won't drag him into it." For a long time she sat there, motionless, rigid, while it got very late; there were footsteps in the corridor and footsteps on the street outside. She could not sleep. She began to feel scared. Her knee was paining her. The stocking was torn at the spot. You could hardly see it in that light. One by one, she began to think of all her sisters in their home in Montreal, one by one, remembering little things about them, their clothes, their hair, their voices, and she wanted to see every one of them before she died.

"Why do I have to think of dying? I'm not going to die." But she was even more scared and she tried eagerly to think again of Father Dowling; but now there were flowing within her all the noises and the cries of that city where she had been born, the noises of the waterfront, the strange guttural voices of drunken sailors calling, softly calling, her fearful going away and her return to the flowing water, the lapping restless heaving water, flowing so steadily in her now and filling her with dread. And at last there floated into her thoughts the face of Father Dowling. She liked to think of his face now, his thick hair and the gentleness in his smile. She began, too, to think of his big, soft, strong hands as if they might hold her and strengthen her even as these thoughts were strengthening her. "I'll never see him again. I'll bet a dollar I never see him again," she thought, and saying this, she was suddenly left without any feeling of security at all as if she were utterly alone. She thought that maybe she might have done something to please him, or even now she might yet do something. She tried to remember one short prayer she had known years ago, but the words came so slowly, the words were fumbled and twisted and she frowned, felt shy and was puzzled by her own feeling as she said, "He knew there wasn't much wrong with me except this."

Shaking her head, she suddenly laughed and jumped up and began to walk up and down the narrow cell. "What on earth was the matter with me sitting there," she thought.

Then she went over to the door and called, "Heh, sweetie." When the policeman on duty came, she put her lips against the bars, smiling, coaxing, "Don't you think you might slip your little girl friend a cigarette?"

"Can't be done, sister," he said.

"Please, darling, not for little me? To little me from little you? Isn't that pretty? It would be like a valentine."

"A few minutes ago you were mighty snooty to us, weren't you. You've changed your tune now," he said.

"Oh, not so much, just a little, but it's still a good tune," she said.

"Well, try and smoke it, then," he said, walking away.

In the morning the two girls were taken to the city hall and put in the cells below the court; later they were brought into the courtroom and sat drooping on a bench by the dock. The woman magistrate, in her black robe, a Mrs. Helen Hendricks, was sitting with her chin cupped in one hand, staring out the window. This woman had been a magistrate for the last five years. It had been felt at the time of her appointment that a woman judge would be more tolerant, or at least more understanding of women than a man would be, but this nervous, severe little woman was often inexcusably harsh. Women dreaded to come before her. There seemed to be some deep restless cruelty within her that often made her savage, particularly when there was a charge of immorality being considered. She often smiled, particularly when some woman tried to faint or grow hysterical, and then she would stand up, lean over the desk and snap, "Stop that sort of thing around here. Try and fool your husband with that sort of nonsense. Don't try and fool me."

The court clerk said, "Catherine Bourassa and Veronica Olsen," and the constable at the door shouted, "Catherine Bourassa and Veronica Olsen," and another policeman outside the door shouted along the corridor, "Catherine Bourassa and Veronica Olsen," all their voices roaring hoarsely, and while all this shouting was being done the girls were sitting beside a sad-looking colored woman charged with vagrancy, a thief from the department stores, a gray-haired member of the Salvation Army and three prim, confident, tired-looking social service workers. When the last voice had echoed outside with their names, the two girls stood up slowly and a constable beckoned them toward the stand. In the courtroom, among the lawyers, the other vagrant women and the constables, Ronnie and Midge looked plain, shabbily dressed and almost unnoticeable. Ronnie had her old red coat thrown over her arm and was standing there in the black silk dress the priest had given her, which was spotted now and badly wrinkled; Midge, too, wore Father Dowling's gray dress and the badly discolored gray shoes.

No one paid much attention to them. There was nothing remarkable about the case. Four similar cases were on the court calendar for that same morning. To the court officials all these women, after a little while, began to look alike. So the magistrate went on staring out the window, waiting, and hardly glanced at Midge and Ronnie. "You are charged with being found in a common bawdy house. How do you plead, guilty, or not guilty?"

"Guilty," they both said, without lifting their heads.

"Just a minute, Your Honor," the court clerk said. "There are others charged along with them. There's a charge of procuring against Lou Wilenski, a charge of keeping a bawdy house against Henry Baer, and a charge of being found in against Raymond Frizzel."

"Bring them in then," the magistrate said. There was once again the loud shouting and echoing of names. First Lou came in with a constable, wearing his green sweater and with his hair combed smooth, glancing around contemptuously at everybody in the court. Among the big policemen he looked even smaller, but this distinction seemed to make him feel all the more independent and stronger. Glancing over at the girls, he smiled once and winked, and then he became perfectly enigmatic.

Still fussing and expostulating, Mr. Baer was insisting the case be adjourned till he could get a lawyer. His black hair still had the sharp white part. His face was quivering with indignation and his glasses helped to make him look like a respectable taxpaying citizen.

When Ronnie saw Lou, she grabbed Midge's arm, her hand began to tremble, she kept muttering, "What have they got against Lou? They're not going to do anything to Lou." For the first time she was suddenly alive, angry and eager. As she stood up, with Midge tugging at her, trying to restrain her, her face had that honest, direct expression that Father Dowling had loved. She wanted to plead with the magistrate and explain that Lou should not be there at all.

The little man with the hatchet face, who never raised his head, willingly gave evidence against the girls, for he understood he would escape without even a fine. He said Lou had met him in the poolroom and had sent him to the hotel and he had given money to Ronnie. While he was speaking an extraordinary viciousness crept into his voice; he wanted to hurt the girls so deeply they would never forget him. His face lit up triumphantly when he finished, for he knew he would be free. Then he added hastily, for fear of forgetting something, "That man," pointing at Mr. Baer, "was at the hotel desk and he pointed to the stairs and said, 'Go up there'."

"Is there any previous conviction against these girls?" the magistrate asked.

"Last year they were convicted of similar offences, Your Honor."

"You've been here before, then?" she said to the girls.

"Yes, ma'am," they said.

"Old offenders," she said. "Back as usual."

The tips of her fingers were caressing her plump chin as she said, "The most horrible offence here was on the part of the man who was procuring. He's little better than the scum of the earth. There's no previous conviction against him but I'm going to send him down for three months. The city is well rid of such rattlesnakes."

Then Ronnie screamed, "That's not fair to Lou. He's done nothing to nobody. He's never been in trouble. He's a good man. He never treated anybody bad. Look at his face. Look at him standing there, ma'am. He's full of kindness. Please, ma'am, you don't know him like I do. If he's done anything it's my fault, because I got him to do it and he did it for me." Ronnie started to cry as she pleaded with the magistrate, who only smiled and said, "My goodness, girl, what eloquence for such a wastrel." And then she went on, "You, Veronica Olsen, where do you come from?"

"Detroit, Your Honor."

"And you, Catherine Bourassa?"

"Montreal, ma'am."

The magistrate, with her chin on her hand, looked at the girls wearily, peering steadily into their faces, trying to find something special about them; the little dark one, she thought, might have been graceful at one time, for even now there was an odd, almost amused bit of a smile hovering around her mouth, though her eyes were wide, soft and scared. From the great window the strong morning sunlight came in a thick shaft across the room and struck the upturned pale, tired face of the tall angular girl; and when the magistrate saw Ronnie's face in this light, full of misery, pleading now because of Lou, she thought the girl looked awkward and ugly. "They're both very commonplace, it seems to me," the magistrate was thinking. "I can't see why anybody should mention those two to me. Why did anybody bother speaking to me about them and intimating what disposition ought to be made of their case? It's beyond me." They seemed to fit so easily into that long procession of girls that kept straggling before her every morning, making her disgusted and angry. "I'd never remember them if I saw them again," she thought.

"I'm going to give you girls till this afternoon some time to get out of town," she said. "I'm going to hand you over to the custody of the Salvation Army to see that you're put on trains. You must never come back here again, or you'll be taken into custody at once. Do you hear? Take them away now."

Eighteen

IN THE EARLY evening Father Dowling went to the hotel. He had borrowed ten dollars from Father Jolly. As he went along the street the feeling of early spring weather softening the night air delighted him and made him walk faster.

When he rapped on the white door, as he had so often done, and waited, with no one answering, he could really feel the emptiness in the room on the other side of the door, feel the darkness there, too, and that the time he had so often dreaded had come at last, when he would keep on knocking and waiting and knocking with no hope of an answer. He tried the knob, the door swung open and he stepped into the room. A little moonlight, coming through the window, shone on the trampled and mussed-up carpet, on the dresser where there was no comb, nor looking-glass, nor small vase, nor brush, nor powder puff. He did not turn on the light because he knew with certitude that there was no one there and yet he called out, "Midge, Ronnie, Midge, Ronnie," and he walked over to the window and then back again, as if his presence alone might make the room seem not so empty.

Gripping the banister, he went downstairs, thinking, "Something has happened to them. They would not go like that. Something dreadful must have happened," and he looked over eagerly at the desk. No one was there. He called out, "Hello, hello, hello there," and he pounded the desk with his fist.

"Just a minute," Mr. Baer called. Coming out, he stared at Father Dowling through his glasses without speaking, staring as if it would never be necessary to see the priest again, and then he snapped, "You get the hell out of here, you fornicatin' friar, and never come back. I've got a hunch you're the cause of a lot of trouble."

"Shut up. Don't talk so much. Where are the two girls?"

"I told you to get on your horse. Didn't you hear me?"

"Where are those girls? Have you put them out?"

"I'm putting you out, Lovin' Sam, you understand? You been sneaking in and out of here grinning like a baboon and drawing a crowd. We might just as well of hired a band as let you in. Now I'm going to let the whole neighborhood know how you've been whacking away at those girls. How will you like that, Lovin' Sam?"

For the first time Mr. Baer was sneering openly at the priest, his lower lip hanging thickly after he spat with vicious contempt. Father Dowling felt and remembered all those times when he had tried to hide his collar; he felt all the secret smirking that had followed him every time he came into the hotel, all those times when he had gone upstairs with his back to the desk, with the man's eyes following and an ugly grin on his face. That leering contempt which had remained hidden in Mr. Baer was made plain now when he spat contemptuously.

"I asked you where the girls were," Father Dowling shouted, and he shot his hand across the desk and grabbed Mr. Baer by the collar. Father Dowling was a big, powerful man. His face now was hard and brick red, the lips sucked in so there was only a colorless line at his mouth. He kept shaking Mr. Baer by the neck, holding him even while the eyes bulged. "What happened to those girls, you foul-mouthed swine?" he was saying.

"Let me tell you," Mr. Baer gasped.

"Hurry."

"Take your hand off my throat, Father."

"There. Hurry up now, or I'll knock some respect into you, you lizard."

"The kids were pinched last night. The cops raided the place. They pinched me, too. They pinched Lou, Father."

"Where are the girls now? Why are you here?"

"The kids had to get out of town or go to jail, and they fined me two hundred and fifty bucks and I haven't made a cent for three years, and God knows what I'll do now."

"You don't know where the girls went?"

"I'd tell you if I did, Father. I don't know where they've gone and they were fine kids, too, no trouble at all."

Out on the street, Father Dowling suddenly felt that there was no place for him to go. He looked up and down the street. A little piece of paper by the curb, caught in a gust of wind, went spinning and eddying along the road till it was out of sight. "Where will they go? What will become of them?" he was thinking.

When he went home, he met Father Jolly. The little, thin-faced priest with the glasses started to laugh as soon as he saw him and he said, "Things are coming your way at last. I'm being moved out of town. I'll give you my room by a last will and testament. The room with the nice shelves for your books. The room you always coveted with a lustful eye."

"Thanks, Father. Sorry you're going."

"What's the matter with you? Aren't you glad about the room?"

"It's a fine room. I'll be glad to get it."

"Is something bothering with you? I thought you'd be chuckling with joy."

But Father Dowling did not hear him. He went up to his own room. He took off his shoes and put them together on the floor and stared at them thoughtfully. "I'll go to the city hall to-morrow. I'll find out something." He got undressed and lay wide awake in bed. "They needed me very much. Who will help them now? What is there for them to do?" he was thinking.

Nineteen

IN THE MORNING, after he had said a mass for the soul of Mrs. Schwartz, who was being buried that day, Father Dowling went down to the city hall to try and find out where the girls had gone. They sent him to the probation office, where there might be some record, they said. The polite, lazy-moving, white-haired probation officer, a Mr. Woolf, was very glad to see the priest, for he would welcome any one into his office who would sit down and listen to him telling about his remarkable cases. "Sit down, Father," Mr. Woolf said and he started a long, amiable conversation while Father Dowling waited impatiently with his head thrust forward, almost pleading with the man to stop talking and look into his records. But the probation officer, seeing the intense eagerness in the young priest's face, thought this was a splendid opportunity to describe the variety and scope of his work. "Do you know, Father, in this probation office, in this little black book, we have the names of some of the finest people in town, husbands who can't get along with their wives, wives being given another chance, and so on. You'd be surprised, that's all I say," he said, tapping the little black book lovingly.

"But have you any record of these two girls? Two girls who were in our parish," Father Dowling interrupted apologetically. He leaned forward. "They were arrested the other day and, I believe, told to get out of town. They told me you might be keeping track of them."

"What did you say their names were, Father?"

"Midge Bourassa and Ronnie Olsen."

"Nothing recently, Father. If they were told to get out of town they'd really be getting out of our jurisdiction." While Father Dowling leaned over the desk, moistening his lips, still hoping desperately that some small fact might yet be discovered, the officer started to thumb through his book. "A year or so ago there was a mention of those two names. Two little streetwalkers. It was hard to keep in touch with them when they were on probation. We lost track of them. What were they like?"

"One was a little dark girl with a kind of impish way about her. The other was tall and rather severe in her way." Father Dowling was standing up and indicating with his hand the height of the girls, and when he paused, with his lips parted, he seemed ready to go on and describe their faces.

"You had a very deep interest in them, Father?"

"I've been trying to help them for some time."

Looking closely at the young priest, Mr. Woolf really felt sorry for him, for when he first came in he had been so hopeful and apologetic; now he wanted to stand there and keep on describing the girls, so they would suddenly become so real one would have to remember them.

"I'm sorry. I don't remember them," Mr. Woolf said.

As he walked away from the city hall, Father Dowling saw no one else on the street in the spring sunlight; the images of the two girls alone filled his thoughts. "I ought to have done something for them more than I did. They were like children. I know what will happen to them. Lord, be kind to them, be merciful to them. They'll drift into the old way of life. They'll go from one degradation to another, they'll be poor and hungry and mean. No one will ever love them for themselves. No one will ever want to help them and they'll get harder and harder till they'll be immune to all feeling. Why should they be without the love of some one? Why should I not have been allowed to help in the way I could?" He walked along the street pondering the matter, thinking that God's justice was mysterious. It seemed to him as he frowned and hung his head that the girls were being deliberately abandoned. Then he straightened up and thought, "I shouldn't say that. That's blasphemy. They're abandoned from my help. Surely not from the mercy of God." This comforted him. He walked more easily with the strong city sunlight shining on his face that was now almost confident and trustful. It was even more comforting to him to realize that Easter time was coming, the most joyous period of the whole year. When he passed a corner where men were working on a building and heard the tap-tap-tap of riveters, the sharpness of the noise was startling. He looked up, and again he was thinking, "They'll be lost to all human goodness. What will become of them?"

Before dinner, when Father Dowling was reading the newspaper, young Father Jolly came in and said to him, "Poor Mrs. Schwartz, she's buried now. God rest her soul. How did she die?"

"A most beautiful death," Father Dowling said, putting down his paper. "I've rarely seen such peace. It was a beautiful death."

"It was very bad up at the cemetery, it rained so heavily last night. The ground was terribly muddy after the winter snow."

"Was it still raining at the time of the burial?"

"No. It had stopped. I don't like the rain at funerals. I like there to be sunshine."

"This is the rainy season. You can't have much sunshine in the winter, either."

"No, but then you have snow. Snow is different. Well, the poor soul's gone. I'm glad she died so well. God give her peace," Father Jolly said. "She'll go straight to heaven as far as I'm concerned," and he nodded his head with absolute certainty.

Father Dowling raised his newspaper, but he went on thinking of the departed soul of old Mrs. Schwartz. Her soul was in such peace and so well secured. He glanced again at the newspaper; two young men had held up a girl and robbed her of her purse. A young mother had tried to kill herself and her child because they were without food and a place to live. This spring there were floods in China and talk of war all over Europe, and there were riots in Germany and a hunger march on London. It was the same all over. In Canada one-third of the workers had no jobs. All the street sounds, the rattle of cars bringing crowds home from work, the steady throbbing of city life, could be heard quite clearly. But Mrs. Schwartz had died very beautifully after being so afraid of death on that night when he had first met Ronnie and Midge. Before him, as he listened, there seemed to be slowly passing all those restless souls who were struggling and dying all over without consolation. And these who were living seemed so much more in need of peace and the justice of God than the soul of the dead old lady who had known such repose.

Twenty

ONE AFTERNOON Father Dowling was in the poor neighborhood, visiting Mrs. Canzano, the Italian woman who was very ill, after bearing her twelfth child successfully. This Italian family lived on a street that was a blind alley, in a row of yellow roughcast cottages under one long sagging roof. Father Dowling sat by the woman's bedside. She had the weariest, whitest face he had ever seen, and sometimes her black eyes had a frightened look. "I will not have another child. I'll go mad. I can't stand it. Look at me, Father. The child will die. Why should the child live? They hurt me this time. They were not good to me. I did not want to see the child when they brought it to me. Kids, kids, kids, they just keep coming and I don't know why. It would be different if I knew why. You understand, Father? But nobody knows why?" Her eyes were enormous now in her pinched, hollow face. Her body lay dreadfully still as if she never wanted to move again after the birth struggle. When the young priest was patting her hand and speaking very soothingly she started to cry. Beside her lay the purple-faced child, with round eyes which now began to glow and snap brightly. The child's small hand wriggled with life, and Father Dowling smiled. The mother looked at the child and smiled, too, patting the hand that stirred.

Eight of the other children were still alive. Three of them were out playing on the street. Two girls were standing at the foot of the bed and the priest shuddered because there was a fixed silliness in their eyes. While he was talking, the husband came in, a short, fierce-looking little man wearing a blue denim shirt, and carrying parcels of food in his arms, for he was on city relief and had just come from the city food kitchens.

"Good afternoon, Mr. Canzano," Father Dowling said warmly. "God has been good enough to give you another child."

"God is not good to do such a thing," the Italian said sharply, shaking his head with violence.

"You must not say that. You must believe in God, Mr. Canzano."

"I believe in God, but he is not good," the Italian said. "You know that."

"You must not despair like that, Mr. Canzano."

"I do despair, Father. We must despair. What else is there for us to do? Look at my wife. Look at me. You understand, Father? There is nothing left but despair," and leaning forward intently, he shook his hand erratically at the priest. His hand kept on shaking and he seemed to have forgotten about it; the hand seemed to be detached from his body. "I'll pray hard for you," Father Dowling said. "I should not have mentioned the child," he thought. "There may be much that we don't understand," he added awkwardly. But he got up to go in a hurry, for he felt he must have appeared complacent, and he pitied the man and woman so that he dared not rebuke them for their despair. "I'll come and see you again. Just a friendly call. And I'll baptize the baby soon, eh? Keep me out if you don't like to see me," he said, trying to laugh. He went out to the street where the little kids were shouting and playing with a ball. All the kids stopped to watch him coming out of the Italian's house. Some ran up to him as he waved his hand. "Some of the children of that man were not right wise. I could see it in their faces," he thought. "More children while the woman grows more wretched and the man full of despair. God help them. It's inevitable that some of those girls go on the streets and become far worse than Ronnie and Midge." These girls playing on the street suggested a problem to him. What chance did they have for spiritual development when they were born with weak minds? When they died how did God judge their souls? Was it original sin that accounted for their condition? If they were not normal, and therefore, not to be judged, what was the purpose behind their existence? Or was it all something like the problem often raised in old classes in logic, the problem of the two-headed calf that simply couldn't be explained by original sin or in any other satisfactory way.

Then he began to feel that his love for Midge and Ronnie made much more comprehensive his sympathy for all the wretched people he had ever known. "The more I love and think of those girls the closer I am to all these people," he thought, and he felt glad.

But at the close of benediction that evening, when the bell had been rung by the acolyte, and he had replaced the Blessed Sacrament in the tabernacle, and the congregation, having risen, was singing the *Sicut Erat* of the *Gloria*, and he was walking from the altar, he felt the beginning of a fear that almost sickened him. He began to take off his vestments. The altar boys who had assisted him were talking rapidly to each other. There was worry and love and eagerness in his feeling, but mostly fear, as he thought that he was the only one who could have prevented the girls from losing their souls forever; he was the only one who really knew them and loved them; and he began to long to be with them so he could talk to them gently, show them how much he cared for them and encourage them to be patient. He was also thinking that by this time they might have the same terrible despair that was in the angry eyes of the little fierce Italian who had stood in front of him with the parcels of food in his arms.

Father Dowling could go no further in his thoughts without talking to some one. He went into the house, put on his hat and coat and walked up the street to see his friend, Charlie Stewart. Just before he went into the apartment house, he looked up at the light and felt very thankful that he had a friend like the young medical student, who would listen willingly and, no doubt, see the whole matter clearly.

As soon as Charlie Stewart saw Father Dowling he knew he was worried, but he was patient, and he began an involved conversation, a pompous monologue on economics. Father Dowling was bending forward, rubbing the palms of his hands together between his knees. "Something on your mind, Father?" Charlie said suddenly, terminating his conversation and becoming simple and friendly. It was about nine o'clock in the evening. The spring night air was filling the room through the open window. It was the time when Father Dowling had gone so often to the hotel. Very slowly he began to tell about the girls and how he was worrying about them now. He did not talk with the ardor and enthusiasm of that night when he had walked along the street with the lawyer, for sometimes he even halted, looking up anxiously at his friend, and then went on mildly as if explaining his worry to himself.

"Father, that's curious. It does focus a social problem. Why didn't you tell me before?" Charlie Stewart said as he got up and began to walk up and down the room in his enthusiasm. Watching him, Father Dowling thought, "What a splendid fellow he is," and he even felt a fresh warmth in himself. His face began to glow with eagerness because his friend understood his feeling so well.

"If you feel like walking, we could take a walk over to the neighborhood and I'll show you the hotel," Father Dowling said.

The young medical student, who had been so sophisticated, who had discoursed so learnedly on political economy, now seemed to be giving deep consideration to the priest's enthusiasm. They walked along in step through the poor neighborhood; they came to the hotel by the lighted lunch counter. They stood on the other side of the street looking at the hotel with the broken sign, the drab front, the poorly lit entrance. "I've passed this hotel a hundred times, Father," Charlie said. Father Dowling had grabbed his friend's arm tightly, looking over at the hotel, but then he sighed and said, "Probably some other place by this time. There's some other hotel with an entrance just like that. Do you think so, Charlie?"

"It all depends. Not if they think of you at all, Father."

"Do you think they'd remember me occasionally? It would be a wonderful consolation if I could keep thinking they would."

"There must surely have been times, Father, when you felt you had a real effect on them, weren't there?"

"Oh, there were. Times, too, when they didn't know it, and I was delighted. We'll go back and I'll tell you." He told first of all about the time he had brought the money and left it for Midge, and that time when the two girls had come into the room with their new dresses and had looked at him shyly. "They were just like a couple of kids. You ought to have seen them. They didn't know how they looked," he said. There was the time, the last time, when he had come and found them with men and Midge had turned at the door and said simply, "I'm sorry, Father, that you saw me like this." "Seldom have I seen such simple regret," he said. "They could be so warm-hearted and thankful." He told of many other little incidents he must have observed very shrewdly. "Of course, I know they often deceived me. I tried not to be foolish about the matter. They continually deceived me. I see that now. They often hurt me. But it doesn't matter if they wounded my self-respect or my pride a thousand times, does it? They were streetwalkers, Charlie, but they made me think about prostitution."

"If you don't mind me saying it, Father, I disagree with you to a certain extent about these girls," Charlie said. "In the perfectly organized state there would be no streetwalkers. If the state has a proper control of the means of production and the means of livelihood, it's never necessary for a woman to go on the streets. No healthy woman of her own accord would ever do such work. It's too damned degrading. But if in the ideal state there were still women who were streetwalkers out of laziness or a refusal to work steadily then they would be kicked out or interned somewhere for laziness, or as non-producers. Then they'd have to work or starve. Your mistake is seeing this as a religious problem. It's really an economic problem. Do you see, Father?" Charlie said like a lecturer.

"I know, and in a way you're right, but not entirely. I knew a woman who thought all these girls were feeble-minded. All you would have to do would be to sterilize the feeble-minded, and in a couple of generations everything would be rosy for the strong-minded ones, who would all be highly moral. It's a point of view."

"It's not my point of view."

"No. I've been trying to see it in this way. I wouldn't say it to everybody, Charlie, but I know many respectable women in the parish enjoying marriages of convenience and I know they're just as low in the scale as these girls. I mean when you think of the girls hunting around the streets here and the young men and the married men going to them because of their secret passion and their lust, it looks almost as if the girls, even here in my own parish, were in a way doing some good – in a way, had a spiritual value. These girls were taking on themselves all these mean secret passions, and in the daytime those people who had gone to them at night seemed to be leading respectable and good lives. Those girls never suspect the sacrifice of their souls that they offer every day. I know Father Anglin would not agree with me on this point. I am not sure about it. I've just been trying to understand it myself. All I'm driving at is that we get so accustomed to despising those girls that we never see them at all. I'll think more about it, Charlie, and we'll talk it over, eh?" Then he was silent. Charlie Stewart, too, was silent for a while, for he saw that Father Dowling was trying to find something in the girls' lives that was good. He said impulsively, "Maybe we could find out where those girls are gone, Father. We'll find out where they are gone and you can write them or go and see them."

"I'll try and think of some way of doing it. You try too, Charlie, will you?" the priest asked. "Please try hard."

Then there was hardly any more conversation, and

Charlie knew the priest was worrying about the life the girls might now be leading.

After he had left his friend, Father Dowling went into the deserted church. He stood in the aisle looking up toward the red sanctuary light. He walked on tiptoe in the aisle of the deserted church as if some slight noise, or a footfall, might disturb its peace. In the darkness the white altar gleamed brightly. With his eyes on the tabernacle, he knelt down, blessing himself, his face full of timidity, and he began to pray to the Virgin Mary. He asked the Blessed Virgin to be a mother to the two girls because of her own virginity. Closing his eyes, he began a contemplation of the mystery of Mary's virginity. And then, with his eyes closed, he was making no conscious prayer, using no word; his mind was swept clear of all thoughts so there was only a void and a darkness within him. But this most silent prayer was more intense than any he had ever made.

Twenty-one

FOUR DAYS before Easter the Bishop sent for Father Dowling. The Bishop's huge, dark, solemn face with the swift-moving eyes showed a little irritation when Father Dowling came into the library and kissed his ring. He withdrew his hand too hastily. Of course, a bishop rarely gave anybody an opportunity actually to kiss his ring. Usually he put out his hand and withdrew it just when some one was bowing low over it.

Father Dowling, who had expected to hear from either the Bishop or Father Anglin ever since he had taken the girls to Robison's house, had come eagerly, sure that his explanation would be understood, and even now, looking at the Bishop's crimson stock below his white collar, some of his hopefulness was still animating him. He stood still, with his hands stiffly at his sides.

The Bishop's double chin folded softly as he drooped his head, staring for a long time without speaking as though he had never seen Father Dowling before and was trying now to make up his mind about him. There was something so direct, simple and confident about the young priest that the Bishop grew even more irritated. "Perhaps you know why I wanted to see you, Father Dowling?" he began mildly. "Have you any idea?"

"I would not like to say, Your Grace."

"You've been in the company of two girls a good deal recently."

"Yes, Your Grace."

"Common prostitutes."

"Yes, Your Grace."

There had been a little smile on Father Dowling's face but the way the Bishop said common prostitutes hurt him, and his face reddened with resentment and hostility toward the Bishop. Then he was ashamed, knowing that in looking closely at the Bishop, peering into his puzzling, mysterious, heavy face which never revealed his thoughts, and not liking the slight almost rolling motion of one heavy lip on the other, he was looking critically at him, as he would at an ordinary man, instead of simply seeing him as his superior, and accepting his words on these matters as he would the word of God.

"Are you about to object, Father?" the Bishop said.

"No, Your Grace."

"I've heard you've been going continually to this hotel and seeing these girls and giving them things and staying with them nearly all night, and being seen on the street with them, and so on. You may have some explanation. I'd like to hear it, but it seems to me you've been deliberately courting scandal, scandal in a community where we are in a minority, Father, and where the life of a priest in these matters must be above reproach." The Bishop drawled these last words out, his voice going nasal, slow and a bit sarcastic. "I believe, of course, that you started out to help these girls, that's true, isn't it, Father?"

"I started out to help them, Your Grace. I kept on helping them. I was helping them up to the time they were arrested."

"Helping them how, Father?"

"Helping them with my presence." If only the Bishop wouldn't drawl his words out so slowly, Father Dowling was thinking. The way he asked, "Helping them how?" made Father Dowling suddenly wonder about everything he had tried to do. The simple question was somehow destructive of his faith in himself, but he said boldly, "I was helping them by my presence. I tried to be with them as much as possible."

"Were you having any effect, do you think?" the Bishop asked with real curiosity. There was a bit of wonder in his voice now, as if he really wanted to believe Father Dowling had helped the girls.

"I was trying to keep them off the streets. There were many times when they delighted me with a bit of feeling, sometimes hard to describe, Your Grace, but filling me with hope."

"But when you wanted to get them, you knew where to look for them. On the streets, eh?"

"I know the girls often deceived me, Your Grace, but does it matter that they did? I don't think so. Supposing they deceived me again and again. Was I to become impatient or weary, or abandon them, out of disappointment? Your Grace, I've thought of the matter a good deal. I can't understand how we, or the whole race, can ever hope for justice, or can expect to go forward, or can hope for absolution if we can't see that even our dreams disappoint us. Even a dream of social betterment usually is a bitter disappointment. We've got to accept the disappointment and go on. All of us must be terribly disappointing to God. By any standard of justice God might have abandoned us all long ago and left us to shift for ourselves as those girls are shifting now wherever they are, whatever they are doing."

"Just a moment, Father. We're not discussing those matters now. I'm simply telling you that you were giving scandal. I'm not arguing with you."

"I understand, Your Grace."

"Weren't you tempted, being continually exposed to a life of temptation?"

"No, Your Grace."

"There was no carnal satisfaction, Father?"

"Not that I know of, Your Grace."

The Bishop seemed to become more sullen than ever but really it was only that his conscience was bothering him. One part of his mind was telling him that the young priest was utterly without blame; the other part of his mind was urging him to be rational, to be firm, to administer his office according to his highest conception of duty. While he was looking so sullen and uncommunicative, he was fearing that he was softening, yielding to a personal sentiment, or liking the young priest and letting himself meditate on his conduct whereas he knew definitely, as a bishop, that such conduct could not be tolerated in this community. Besides there was also the charity drive throughout the city that would be spoiled by circulation of scandalous stories about priests. "This you can see at least, Father," he said patiently. "Let us say in the beginning when you went to visit those girls you were moved by a kind of divine love. But can't you see how you were drawn into their lives, how you were sucked in and immersed in their lives so your single besetting worry became the comfort and life of those streetwalkers? It became a purely human love, if I may put it in that way. I mean the quality of your interest changed completely."

"Do you mean, Your Grace, that I came to love them for themselves?"

"Yes, so that they themselves were more important than the sinfulness they represented. Let me see how I ought to put it. . . ."

Becoming intensely interested, the Bishop leaned forward, anxious to probe into the matter and discover the nature of this love, to see it objectively as a philosophical problem.

"Yes, I did grow to love them for themselves," Father Dowling said.

"Can't you see it was an impossible state of affairs for you, a priest?"

"It seems to me it was loving them in the only way I knew how, Your Grace."

"Father, as an older priest, let me tell you something. It was a form of arrogance on your part to think you could go on with that relationship. Do you understand now?"

"I do not understand that aspect of it. Those girls have

been arrested and sent away. They will live now as thousands of other prostitutes live till they grow old, then they'll just be old prostitutes with nothing to do."

Smiling, the Bishop said, "I believe they were living that way now, anyway," but he was thinking "He's still worried about them. He's still absorbed in their lives. It won't do at all." Then he said, "I should imagine the notion of prostitution alone would make you sick with disgust."

"If I start hating prostitutes where am I going to stop?" Father Dowling asked. "These girls have prostituted their bodies. All around us there are all kinds of people prostituting their souls and their principles for money. I know people in this city who prostitute our faith for the sake of expediency. I watch it going on all around and wonder how corrupt our faith can become before it dies. So if I can't have charity for those girls, certainly I can have no love for many others in higher places."

The Bishop saw that he was making no impression on Father Dowling with his arguments so he said impatiently, "I've tried to state the matter clearly. I say you can't go on in this way. You'll have to obey me in this matter."

"I will do whatever Your Grace advises."

"Except agree with me, eh? I'll have to think of something to do about it most certainly, something in the way of discipline. You ought to be taken away from here."

"If you think it best, Your Grace."

"That's all, Father."

Father Dowling's smooth skin was flushed with embarrassment. Almost pleading for some informal conversation, he looked anxiously at the Bishop, who was fussing with some papers on his desk. "Good afternoon, Your Grace," Father Dowling said.

"Good afternoon, Father." The Bishop put out his hand laconically as if the conversation had lost its importance for him.

There was such a nervous trembling in Father Dowling when he left the Bishop's palace that he found it hard to think at all. A fearful disappointment was shaking him, and this came from knowing that he would be disciplined like a fallen priest, or like one who was simply not a good priest. His mother would be expecting him home for Easter, too. Then he grew calmer and more meditative, for he was thinking, "Obedience is necessary. Obedience is to be preferred even to sacrifice." In his spiritual reading he had learned that sacrifice was always much easier than obedience. As he reached the corner and stood looking across at a drug store, he knew that in his thoughts he could not obey the Bishop and this disturbed him. He decided to go into the drug store and have a soft drink and he sat there staring at the marble counter, blinking his eyes and pondering his wilful lack of obedience. The Bishop had said that his love had degenerated. "How could God have loved those girls if not for themselves? How otherwise then could I have loved them?" he asked himself. And if God was able to love all souls without distinction in His divine way in spite of their failures, their lusts and avariciousness and their miserable condition, wasn't he, a simple priest, through his love of these two girls, loving the whole world, too? He began to smile, and he felt very confident with a swift rush of marvellous joyfulness.

Twenty-two

THAT EVENING the Bishop's spiritual adviser had come to hear his confession. The Bishop was kneeling down on a plush footstool conducting an examination of his conscience and the plump fingers of one big hand were folded softly over the other hand that held a rosary. His heavy head was hanging on the side and his eyes kept opening slowly, then remaining shut for some time. As he prayed his lips made a whispering sound, and when he drew in his breath it was like a thin whistle. Over and over he kept questioning himself about every sin he might have committed in the last week. His sins seemed to be so few that he was alarmed and groped anxiously for more, knowing he could not be without guilt. He asked himself if he had always been charitable in his transactions. Whenever the Bishop was worried about his failure to see his sins clearly, he charged himself with a consistent lack of charity. "Have I been harsh in my judgments? Have I dwelt upon the faults of others? Have I been arrogant in my office?" he asked himself. More than anything else the Bishop dreaded the spiritual complacency that was often the lot of some good men in the priesthood. His enormous shoulders were drooping and his dark impassive face was full of perplexity as he tried to strip away all concealment till he would be as frank with himself as a little child. In the course of a long consideration of his judgments he finally thought of Father Dowling and the way he had rebuked him. Suddenly the carefully tabulated points in his examination of conscience went out of his head; he began to think of himself as a young priest, he remembered the time when he had been young, slim, extraordinarily tall and had longed to love Christ in everything he did; he remembered how he had trembled with joy that day when he had finished saying his first mass, and how slow, laconic and indifferent the older priests had appeared, how their patient smiles had seemed to come out of spiritual inertia. This ardor had lasted him many years and nothing else had been necessary but to abandon himself to his own good intentions, and then as he had grown older he had become more intellectual, more cautious and had formed estimates of the value of all human actions. "I never was so happy as when I was a young priest, not much younger than Father Dowling," he thought.

It was then that he realized he was thinking of Father Dowling as though he loved and wanted to help him. This startled the Bishop. "Don't I believe in my own actions? I know he was giving scandal. There was nothing else to do. He must be sent away, probably to a monastery. I don't have to go over all that again." But he couldn't help feeling that he, judging the young priest, might not have been without some kind of sin in the matter. "Father Dowling made a fool of himself. It became a kind of arrogance in him. Who does he think he is to win those girls over just by his presence?"

A feeling stronger than his reason was urging him that his doubt and perplexity was a matter for his spiritual adviser. He seemed to be trying to grip and hold his own conscience, refusing to let himself reconsider his judgment of Father Dowling. "My own conscience must give me the answer in these questions," he thought. "If it is not so then it is impossible for me to administer my office." And he tried to start praying again. He began to move his lips rapidly with the words of a prayer flowing steadily out of him. "But how could Father Dowling have been successful with the girls?" he asked himself suddenly. "What might he have done? It's absurd. He would have to have been a saint. I don't know much about him. It's odd I've never really heard of him before," he whispered.

The Bishop, who thought he was ready now to make a good confession, closed his eyes, became silent, ready to stand up, and then it came into his head again, "Father Dowling in the beginning may have loved them in a general way and, of course, that was good. His love for them became too concrete. How could it become too concrete? From the general to the particular, the conception expressed in the image." It seemed to become a kind of philosophical problem for the Bishop and he was groping for an abstract statement. "From the word to the flesh, the word made flesh, from the general to the particular, the word made flesh, no, no, nonsense . . . then the general made concrete . . . no, no." But the Bishop could not meditate at all now and had become angry with himself. "What is the matter with me? Do I feel I suffer from the sin of hardness of heart?" he muttered. He knew he would have to wait for another mood, a more peaceful frame of mind before going to confession, and he got up slowly, his knees feeling stiff. Up and down the room he paced restlessly, feeling sure that as a rational man there had been only one way to consider the question of Father Dowling's conduct. "If I had it to do over again, I would face the problem in exactly the same way," he thought firmly. "What on earth is bothering me then? He was an honest man who committed himself to a piece of folly that can't be tolerated, that's all there is to it."

The Bishop paced up and down irritably in this way, muttering to himself about Father Dowling, while his spiritual adviser was still waiting to hear his confession.

Twenty-three

THAT EASTER was a fine clear sunlit day, the warmest day of the year, when the crowds poured into church wearing their new garments, and the altars were decked with fresh lilies and green stuff, and the great choir tried to sing better than ever before. As he made his preparations for mass Father Dowling suddenly wondered if it could be that the bodies of Midge and Ronnie were being destroyed as the bread and wine in the mass would be destroyed, so that God could enter in in the mystery of transubstantiation. "The death of Christ, the life of souls," he thought, and was full of hope as he passed through to the altar. In his gold and white vestments, Father Dowling looked very handsome saying mass, for the altar lights gleamed on his black hair and the two little boys serving mass for him and holding the edges of his cape made him look taller than ever.

After mass he went down to the church door, but he stood almost out of sight of people as if he feared that already they were talking about him. He was standing where he could see at least the crowd streaming out to the sidewalk, and where he could look with great eagerness at the bright faces of young girls, the fresh smooth young faces full of contentment, all the girls wearing their new Easter clothes in so many vivid colors. They all looked beautiful to him. But by the time the last few stragglers had reached the door and were looking up lazily at the intensely blue sky and the strong sunlight, Father Dowling had become very grave. He was thinking that to-day, as on every Easter Sunday, there was a kind of freshening and quickening in the parish girls because it was the most joyful season of the year, but with Midge and Ronnie, even though they did not realize it, it was still the hard dark time of the Good Friday passion.

At the noonday meal he wanted very much to have lively conversation and some laughter, so he started a conversation with Father Jolly about the increasing number of mixed marriages in the parish. He gave it as his opinion that a Catholic girl, marrying a Protestant, often succeeded in bringing him into the Church. But he was interrupted by the old priest saying, "I think you have the wrong attitude altogether to these matters. I think you ought to get straightened out on them." There was Father Anglin, old and irritable, and growing more untidy every day, fifty years in the priesthood, with his face heavy and pink and his eyes clear and stern from fifty years of unrelenting acceptance of authority, implying by his tone his sharp disapproval and his awareness of the discipline for the young priest that the Bishop was planning. His dreadful uncomprehending primness was overawing; like many another severe old priest, he felt a little like a pope and was ready to excommunicate in his own militant mind all who disagreed with him.

Father Dowling resented the harsh criticism that was in the old priest's eyes, but he said nothing; he remained silent with his head lowered. He knew that from now on every small disagreement he had ever had with the old priest would be intensified and that from now on they would probably watch him, too. They would ponder over everything he said. They would watch him at night and in the daytime, too, as they did a priest whose conduct had been questioned. Already even, he believed that many people knew in the parish that he was to be sent away, for he realized how rapidly stories about priests spread in a parish. Father Jolly had an aunt living in the neighborhood;

she would receive just the faintest intimation from her nephew that Father Dowling was in trouble; for days she would try desperately not to mention the matter to anybody and finally would whisper it to a dear friend and then plead that it be told to no one else.

A sharp awareness of all these things was in Father Dowling as he sat silent with his head lowered at the dinner table and heard the old priest talking to Father Jolly. But since he had decided that his love for the girls was good, he did not care what they said about him. "I only wish I had more love to give them. I dare not look for them," he thought. He began to think of his love as a steady prayer that would grow more fervent from day to day, and at one moment, when he raised his head from the table, he looked so eager, and at another time, so worried, that the priests stopped talking and stared at him.

That evening he had a letter to write home to his mother, a very difficult letter that he had been avoiding the last two days. He sat in his room and pondered and wrote, "You would not believe how busy I have been and how few moments I have had to myself. Father Jolly is being moved out of town. It is a great disappointment that I will not be home at all during Easter week but I will be thinking of you steadily." It was not a good letter, but he wanted to conceal any intimation of his own uneasiness, and it was written three times. "She's a very shrewd woman. She'll start having her own thoughts. Sooner or later she'll hear something," he thought, and he began to dread hearing from his mother and his brother.

He sat at his desk with his head in his hands, worrying, thinking of his brother meeting him at the station, remembering the Sunday turkey dinner they had and the bottle of wine and the neighbors who came in and sometimes brought gifts, remembering the way the sunlight shone on the slopes of the blue hills; and then without feeling any other flow in his thoughts, he began to see the face of Midge and sometimes the face of Ronnie, and he began to feel that even by this time their faces would be more hardened and vicious. So again he wanted his love to be like a prayer. He remembered the night he had prepared his sermon out of the Song of Solomon, and he got up and looked for the book and began to read the Song again. He read with his face beginning to glow; he seemed to understand more deeply every passionate avowal of love. "We have a little sister with no breasts, what shall we do for our little sister?" he read, and he smiled. "At night on my bed I sought her whom my soul loveth . . ." It seemed to Father Dowling as he sat at his desk with the city noises of that spring night coming through the window that he understood this love song as it had never been understood before, that each verse had a special, fresh, new meaning for him. "I'll write a commentary on it verse by verse and show how human love may transcend all earthly things," he thought, and this resolution gave him joy and a kind of liberation from the small room. He began to plan his commentary, tapping, tapping very lightly with the pen handle on the desk and sometimes nodding his head. He heard the noises from people moving in the house, but these sounds now did not interest him at all.

Twenty-four

DURING those days when Father Dowling was waiting for the discipline the Bishop had promised, he made no calls among his people. It was not necessary to watch him in the evenings because he did not go out any more. It was not necessary for Father Jolly to shake his little dark head and try and appear good-natured and tolerant in spite of the rumor of scandal and disgrace, for he now had few opportunities for conversation with Father Dowling. It was hard even for Father Anglin to show his disgust and scorn, for Father Dowling avoided him and kept to his room.

Early one evening Charlie Stewart came to see Father Dowling. Night after night he had thought about the two girls, he had wondered how he could help Father Dowling to find them and he had waited to hear from the priest. On this evening when he came to the house, he was full of enthusiasm and ready to spin a fine new social theory and defend it warmly.

The little smiling housekeeper showed him into the waiting-room, a plain room with bad gaudy religious pictures, drab walls and dun-colored curtains. "I wonder why they hate bright colors here," he thought. "Father Dowling said once he would like to wear a bright habit rather than the black he wears. Why do they wear black? I'll bet he hates this room." He waited and the housekeeper returned, still smiling, and she asked him if he would go up to Father Dowling's room. With relief, he followed her, for he had been thinking he might have to sit and talk in the bleak old room where he would feel it was necessary to whisper and guard his words carefully. To-night he felt like speaking with passion. The housekeeper said to him at the top of the stairs, "Father has kept to his room too much lately. You ought to take him for a walk," and then she rapped on the door and Charlie went in.

Father Dowling was sitting at his desk in such a way that there was a stillness in his whole body and a stillness in his face. He looked up at Charlie Stewart and he frowned two or three times, and then he sighed and got up and shook hands. But no matter how he tried to smile cheerfully, the curious stillness remained in his face. "Sit down, Charlie. Wait a minute, I'll get you a cigar." He walked over to a shelf and took down a box of cigars. "An Easter gift from one of my parishioners," he said. "We get many little gifts of this kind, thank the Lord. Maybe I shouldn't ask you to be thankful till you've tried the cigar."

They both began to smoke. Charlie nodded his head. "Not bad at all," he said. Father Dowling nodded approval too and blew a cloud of smoke.

"I've been thinking how we talked that night, you remember, when we walked down to that hotel?" Charlie said. "It was one of the best talks we ever had and we've had some fine talks. I've been wondering what might be done about you getting in touch with those girls. I imagine you'd at least like to try, wouldn't you? I was figuring . . ."

"No, Charlie, I don't think it can be done. There's no use wasting your time, Charlie."

"Of course it can be done, Father."

"I'm afraid I wouldn't be able to use any information you secured. I may be going away for a time," Father Dowling said. He spoke mildly and patiently, but he was plainly worried. He said nothing else. His expression changed slightly till it became an expression of detached sadness. As he went on talking, Charlie was thankful that Father Dowling was listening so intently, although he wished once, when he paused, that the priest was a little more responsive. Father Dowling might just as well not have been in the room at all. Charlie went on talking and then he stopped suddenly and asked, "Aren't you interested, Father?"

Father Dowling might not have heard him, for he didn't turn his head. Charlie said again, "Don't you hear me, Father?" Looking up vaguely, the priest nodded his head and smiled. That detached, depressed, heavy stillness was dulling his eyes.

"Don't you feel well, Father?"

Father Dowling looked up at Charlie as if he had never seen him before. Charlie was scared and he got up to go and he said, "Maybe I'd better see you some other time, Father."

Twenty-five

INSTEAD of sending Father Dowling away for discipline, they took him to the hospital out by the lake. There he had a small white room with a bed and a window that looked out over a wide lawn with new green spring grass, the low red-brick buildings and beyond the buildings and the fields, the great blue lake.

When he first came to the hospital the doctors looked at his teeth and his tonsils and were of the opinion that some local infection was the cause of his malady. But they could find nothing wrong with him, and there he was, depressed, slow-moving and ever unanswering. Sometimes he stood looking at the sunlight on the water, or he would go down to the front steps of the main building and sit down by himself not far from the rest of the patients who were enjoying the fine clear weather. They used to sit there together in the sunlight in the middle of the afternoon as if it was a great garden party to which they had all been invited; they used to move around in the rotunda, bowing to each other and talking charmingly. There was one old woman who wore ancient, long flowing dresses, an old, wide velvet hat and a neat little black jacket. She imagined she was hostess at the garden party for all these people and she kept placing her withered hand lightly on their arms, begging them not to be impatient, for soon tea would be served. Father Dowling puzzled this woman because he sat by himself on the step, his eyes wandered over the grass, he never smiled, and he merely looked up patiently when this woman spoke to him as if he would never be able to understand her. So she apologized to him for the strong sunlight; she had asked the management, she said, to provide umbrellas in many beautiful colors, and she expected them to come at any moment.

There was no wall around the hospital; there were no strait jackets, chains, wristlets, anklets or other implements of restraint. There was only the one building for dangerous patients. Father Dowling was free except that he was held there by an absolute stillness within him. Sometimes he was aroused a little by the blue lake and he watched it when the wind was blowing, the sun glistening on the whitecaps and the waves rolling, endlessly rolling and breaking with the old dull sound on the shore.

In the afternoon when the good patients were on the steps and the ones who were getting well were out hoeing in the garden, there appeared at the window of the brick building on the other side of the lawn the frozen face of a gray mad woman who began to explain patiently in a quavering tone the time of her marriage and the country where she had come from and the city where she had lived, and her voice kept rising as she screamed out the violence she was planning. Her wild voice kept ringing over the lawns. No one on the steps seemed to hear her. Father Dowling walked over by the new ploughed land and he looked a long time at the rich brown fertile soil, heavy and dark and moist, and he looked at the men in the big straw hats, working in the fields, and never raising their heads.

There were a few times when Father Dowling had a normal clarity in his thoughts. The first time came one afternoon, four days after he had come there. He was walking around the grounds when he suddenly realized that his thoughts were dreadfully clear. He walked all over, he talked to the men working in the garden, he spoke to some of the white-jacketed orderlies, he saw for the first time the face of the wretched gray-haired woman, he stood at the furthest extremity of the grounds looking out over the clear lake which was so very blue and calm to-day. "I'm out here because most of the time I'm out of my mind," he thought. "God help me and make me well." And he sat down by himself on the grass and wept.

But when he returned to the pavilion, to the smiling women and polite gentlemen, he talked to them for a long time with compassion till they walked away and left him. Later, after he had eaten, he went to his own small room. It had begun to get dark out. He was still grasping eagerly at his swift thoughts as if they were fresh and new and he could caress them. But then he began to weep again, and soon he began to pray.

He realized that he was mad from worrying about Ronnie and Midge, but his worry and love for them now seemed stronger than ever before. "It must all be to some purpose," he thought. "It must be worth while, even my madness. It has some meaning, some end." And in that quiet room, he wondered where the two girls were and what had become of them; they were among the living, they were moving among those who slowly passed before him, all those restless souls the world over who were struggling and dying and finding no peace; he thought with sudden joy that if he would offer up his insanity as a sacrifice to God, maybe God might spare the girls their souls.

He knelt down in the twilight of the room, with his head just above the window ledge, with his face turned to the lake, and he said fervently, "O my God, accept my sickness and insanity as a sacrifice and I will willingly endure it, and my God, for this sacrifice I ask only that You spare the souls of those two poor girls. Preserve their souls and the souls of all the living who need Your pity and justice. Deliver them from all evil." His hands were clenching the window sill and he remained silent for a long time.

Then he got up and stood looking out over the lake. The water was darkening now. There was a cold light on the water. There were no wave lines, no break, only the soft rise and enormous flow toward him. Growing calmer, he said, "I'm content now. I may have many periods of clarity," and then he thought eagerly, "I can go on with my commentary on the Song of Songs."

There was a peace within him as he watched the calm, eternal water swelling darkly against the one faint streak of light, the cold night light on the skyline. High in the sky three stars were out. His love seemed suddenly to be as steadfast as those stars, as wide as the water, and still flowing within him like the cold smooth waves still rolling on the shore.

Afterword

BY MILTON WILSON

Morley Callaghan's novels somehow resist being written about. As a teller of stories he often seems more concerned with suspending or even perplexing our judgment than with defining exactly how his characters come to behave as they do. Thus, writing a critical comment that claims to explain anything about *Such Is My Beloved* feels like working against the grain. To be sure, there are some big confrontation scenes where positions do get sharply defined and opposed. They happen in the Robisons' drawing room and in court. But after I reread this memorable novel, it is scenes of another sort that stick in my mind as most characteristic, where the shifting details of human behaviour somehow defy the patterns and predictions that readers keep trying to impose on them.

Consider the little scene between Father Dowling and Midge in Chapter 7. It begins as the priest, with money for the two prostitutes in his pocket, eagerly leaps up the hotel stairs two at a time and encounters Midge all prettied up and ready to leave her room for a night on the streets. It ends with Midge and him dozing off in the room together before he suddenly wakes up, glances at her sleeping body, and leaves without disturbing her. Between his entrance and his exit they reach a kind of contact without communication. On Midge's side the scene gives us toe-tapping, shoulder-shrugging, lip-pursing, and other signs of impatience, not to mention outright lies ("I was thinking maybe of going over to the store"), but, long before it's over, an acceptance of his presence too, a kind of relaxed uneasiness. He arouses in her wonder and resentment at the same time. She's able to think "I won't be able to go out" in one breath and add "I don't really want to go out" in the next. She can't figure out what's really on his mind or even what he's saying. Yet she stays with him, this blue-eyed man whom she follows with her eyes at a distance, but also hopes might sit next to her on the bed.

On Father Dowling's side the scene gives us his goodwill, his overwhelming desire to provide this girl with whatever she doesn't and should have. But the goodwill includes plenty of self-deception, and the dialogue touches the funny-bone as well as the heart. A naive compliment from Midge ("You think all people are nice") leads him to correct her via scholastic theology, and in the process "volition" ends up sounding like a dirty word as well as a theological one. He inflates her "lazy good humour" into "a desire to make the immediate eternal or rather to see the eternal in the immediate." But the absurdity and the goodwill somehow mingle without friction, as waiting for Ronnie makes him stay longer and long with this "parishioner." And how does one react when he at last turns over the money, in what must be the first envelope ever used for such a purpose in such a room? Midge stretches her neck, longing to see the bill under its covering, as a payoff on a dresser insists on being a formal offering on an altar.

The novel can't be just a collection of such characteristic scenes. What is its overall action? Stated in the most misleadingly clear-cut terms, this is the story of how a priest goes mad and how a couple of prostitutes go from bad to worse. The two stories are intertwined not just because they cause one another but also because they tend to be worked out in the same terms. The most literal coming together occurs when Lou the pimp plays, in a burlesque version, the role of Dowling the priest, complete with handkerchief tied around his neck as clerical collar. But we hardly need such a reminder. Lou exploits everyone, from his family to

Ronnie, for cash; yet Father Dowling in his own way does no less, and, while the reader may be quite properly moved by the priest's undefinable, unfulfillable, and unquenchable love for the two persons whose well-being has become his life's purpose, it isn't hard to find bribery in the way he treats them.

Then there's that recurrent point of reference, the confessional. It provides the occasion for our most unforgettable moment with Bishop Foley, just after his disciplinary session with the "arrogant" priest. The bishop's uncertainty before making his own confession (has he sinned against Father Dowling or not?), his incomplete struggle to explain how both he and the priest have behaved (we never discover what he finally says to his confessor), are something the perpetually surmising (and never quite certain) reader can share. But I'm thinking more of how Dowling responding to confessions and the girls responding to their customers are juxtaposed. As their fellow-whore Marge says to the priest, "I'll bet you more men go to confession to me than to you." And later, when a youth confesses to fornication with someone whom Father Dowling is convinced must be Ronnie or Midge, the priest can't help seeing a redemptive community purpose in their streetwalking – an idea that keeps growing in his mind until they seem like scapegoats being destroyed for the sins of the world. Long before his asylum days, "the whole city . . . whispering its story" becomes for him "a huge confessional where he could not see the faces" and where the rebelling or condemning voices aren't really confessing at all.

But the most striking confessional scene takes place in the hotel room when Father Dowling comes to apologize for the girls' humiliation at the hands of the Robisons, a confessor seeking forgiveness. Before he reaches their room he collides with one customer coming out and when he gets inside he has to wait, listening to the sounds of sex, for a second customer to finish up next door. The latter finally emerges "beaming with an everlasting satisfaction," shining with new life." Nobody else in the novel ever achieves such complete "contentment" except at times Father Dowling himself. Now he watches angrily as the "big pagan" leaves. In its way, however, this moment of fulfilment anticipates the chapter's concluding moment of peace when, after a long dialogue of mutual misunderstanding and (ultimately) mutual forgiveness, priest and girls unite in eating and drinking and conversation that goes on almost all night. It is their last meeting. I have resisted the temptation to call it their last supper or first communion despite Father Dowling's provocative words about "special graciousness" and the "mysticism" of food. The novel is perpetually tempting the reader to see parallels between everything that happens, to force life into patterns of symbolic action that keep repeating themselves, just as Ronnie calls Mrs. Robison a whore like herself. Callaghan invites awareness of such patterns, but I don't think he entirely wants them. What I imagine him saying in the background is: "This may *look* like a parable, but. . . ."

The "buts" are endless – all those details that refuse to be swept under any patterned carpet. Consider Father Dowling's gift of clothes. Callaghan's early fiction is full of people giving and receiving gifts – I hesitate to call it his "theme of charity." Certainly such a theme is here adulterated almost (but not quite) out of recognition. How are the gifts paid for? Father Dowling has already given the girls money extracted (by dubious pressure) from his friend Charlie Stewart, who really needs it for his prospective bride, towards whom the priest feels a mixture of sympathy and spiritual jealousy. Further money is found by not sending his usual monthly gift to the mother and brother who denied themselves to finance his education for the priesthood. When he meets Charlie's girl he persuades her to act as a kind of model for Ronnie and Midge, whom he calls his "nieces" (the euphemism has a long history). Father Dowling's gifts do ultimately give him another moment of "contentment," but the reader of course knows that their main consequence will be to increase the girls' professional attractiveness, and before delivering the goods he spends much of his time worrying about his life and wondering what his fellow priests might think about that unopened parcel on his bed: "Ah, I must not have such thoughts," he mutters. The charity seems very real; also surrounded by qualifications.

A very different example might be the presentation of Lou the pimp. This little guy trying to be a big-time operator, this forcible-feeble exploiter of everyone who doesn't call his bluff, has predator and loser written all over his features. One of the novel's funniest moments comes in the courtroom when Ronnie, blind with love, cries out, "He never treated anybody bad. Look at his face." But Callaghan refuses to turn Lou into a formula by making him incapable of love. In that other gift-presentation scene, when Ronnie gives Lou a shirt and tie and he tears up the tie and strikes the giver, the final paragraph forces us unexpectedly to confront the possibility that, for all the exploitation and violence, Lou's love for her is just as real as hers for him.

One last "but" concerns Callaghan's minimal prose. The term can apply to his syntax and metaphors, but I'm thinking of his limited vocabulary, his continual repetition of simple key words. Take, for example, "smile" and its relatives. The way everyone keeps smiling in this novel, over and over again (Father Dowling more than anyone else), invites monotony. Imagine a sliding scale, with Mr. Baer's "benevolent considerate smile . . . that included . . . all the desires of the world" or his sneering grin through "heavy wet lips" at one end, and maybe Midge's Mona Lisa smile at the other: she "smiled just a little bit as though he amused her in some way she would never reveal." Father Dowling's own smiles run the gamut from radiant to routine and are perhaps most striking when non-existent or virtually so: "he sat there hardly smiling." Callaghan's repetitions, like his potentially symbolic patterns, set in relief his distinctions or incompatibilities.

What about the novel's developing catastrophe? Priest and girls must be seen, in part, as victims of the Robisons, the bishop, and the police court, or of institutional self-preservation, or of the Depression. Clearly Callaghan has no desire to underestimate the dehumanizing pressures of society. Agonizing over Mr. Cinzano's unanswerable questions, Father Dowling becomes, in his own way, as much of a radical as Charlie Stewart. Although inside the cathedral he may address the Virgin in a "silent prayer . . . more intense than any he had ever made," outside he can look up at its cross with "a cool disgust as if the church no longer belonged to him." But his final madness expresses no thwarted rebellion: it seems more like the ultimate version of a detachment from the persons surrounding him, which we have seen signs of right from the start, Charlie being the initial exception. Even when with Ronnie or Midge his deep personal concern can include that "peculiar, wondering, remote expression in his eyes."

Perhaps the psychological turning-point is that climactic moment after his confrontation with the bishop when he wonders whether his love for the two girls isn't somehow the same as God's love for the whole world, and then smiles confidently "with a swift rush of marvellous joyfulness." What follows seems (at first, anyway) like an anticlimax. After failure with the probation officer he never tries to find the girls again, he tells his family that he won't visit them at Easter, he lets the two priests in his lodging fade into background noise, and all he can do when Charlie comes is look at him "as if he had never seen him before" and smile with a "detached, depressed, heavy stillness . . . dulling his eyes." The last chapter finds him in the asylum by the lake, "ever unanswering" and never smiling. But of course there is something more than anticlimax here. Dowling has moments of clarity, like the one with which the novel ends. These allow him some renewal of compassion for the dispossessed, some hope that his madness may have a sacrificial purpose, even some inspiration to work at his commentary on that stumbling block to biblical interpreters, the love poem calling Song of Songs.

As I finish the novel, I think of his love "flowing within

him like the cold smooth waves still rolling on the shore," but also can't forget the waves that he watches only a couple of pages earlier, "endlessly rolling and breaking with the old dull sound on the shore." That shifting wave image is hard to get hold of quite right. It resists any final meaning. For some readers Father Dowling isn't likely to seem any easier.

BY MORLEY CALLAGHAN

AUTOBIOGRAPHY

That Summer in Paris: Memories of Tangled Friendships with Hemingway, Fitzgerald, and Some Others (1963)

DRAMA

Season of the Witch (1976)

FICTION

Strange Fugitive (1928)
A Native Argosy (1929)
It's Never Over (1930)
No Man's Meat (1931)
A Broken Journey (1932)
Such Is My Beloved (1934)
They Shall Inherit the Earth (1935)
Now That April's Here and Other Stories (1936)
More Joy in Heaven (1937)
The Varsity Story (1948)
The Loved and the Lost (1951)
Morley Callaghan's Stories (1959)
The Many Colored Coat (1960)
A Passion in Rome (1961)
A Fine and Private Place (1975)
Close to the Sun Again (1977)
No Man's Meat and *The Enchanted Pimp* (1978)
A Time for Judas (1983)

Our Lady of the Snows (1985)
The Lost and Found Stories of Morley Callaghan (1985)
A Wild Old Man on the Road (1988)

FICTION FOR YOUNG ADULTS
Luke Baldwin's Vow (1948)

MISCELLANEOUS
Winter [photographs by John de Visser] (1974)